MY LONELY BILLIONAIRE

by

SERENITY WOODS

Copyright © 2021 Serenity Woods
All rights reserved.
ISBN: 9798779039758

DEDICATION

To Tony & Chris, my Kiwi boys.

CONTENTS

Chapter One 1
Chapter Two 7
Chapter Three 13
Chapter Four 20
Chapter Five 27
Chapter Six 34
Chapter Seven 41
Chapter Eight 47
Chapter Nine 57
Chapter Ten 63
Chapter Eleven 70
Chapter Twelve 76
Chapter Thirteen 83
Chapter Fourteen 90
Chapter Fifteen 96
Chapter Sixteen 104
Chapter Seventeen 111
Chapter Eighteen 117
Chapter Nineteen 125
Chapter Twenty 130
Chapter Twenty-One 133
Chapter Twenty-Two 139
Chapter Twenty-Three 145
Chapter Twenty-Four 152
Chapter Twenty-Five 160
Chapter Twenty-Six 167
Epilogue 173
Newsletter 178
About the Author 179

Chapter One

Noah

There are two hundred and forty-three steps on the way from my house down to the beach. Seventy-seven planks of wood in the fence by the path. Sixteen large rocks where the path meets the sand.

I know this because I count them every day. It's a kind of meditation as I walk my two German Shepherds. Spike, whose rear legs rest in a doggy wheelchair after the accident that damaged his spine, has trouble navigating the last step onto the beach, and Willow, his best friend, leaps around him while I help him down as if to say, "Come on, slowcoach!"

Today, the first day of July, the blustery wind tugs at my scarf, and I shove my hands deeper into my pockets as I walk along the sand. They call it the winterless north up here in the Northland of New Zealand, which is kind of accurate; it never snows, and we only see a couple of frosts a year, but it's still cool in the mornings and evenings. I like this time of year, though, and days like this are amazing, with clouds scudding across the cornflower-blue sky, and white horses riding the waves onto the shore.

Willow spots a seagull picking at shells in the distance and tears off, barking, and Spike runs after her, his wheels carving the sand into a pattern of wavy lines. I smile, pick up a stone, and throw it as hard as I can. It arcs into the air before falling, and is swallowed up by the churning waves.

Not for the first time, I imagine what it would feel like to be that stone. To sink into the sea, and let it drag me down to its dark depths, where there would be no more pain, no more sadness, nothing but welcome oblivion.

And those fish with the scary bulging eyes and sharp teeth. Maybe not.

Sliding my hands back into my pockets, I keep on walking.

I've a lot on my mind today. It's super busy at the animal sanctuary at the moment. The cyclone that hit us three weeks ago devastated Ward Seven—the room where we keep animals recovering from operations, and we're having that whole end of the complex rebuilt and enlarged. In a way it was a blessing, because we'd exceeded our capacity after only a few years, and it means we're redesigning it, including a much larger recovery room, expanding the grooming center, and creating proper boarding kennels where people can leave their pets while they're on vacation, knowing they're being well cared for.

In thirty minutes, I have a meeting with the architect and the heads of each department to go over the plans. The building firm has all but cleared the site and they're going to be ready to start on the new buildings soon, so we need to make sure we're all clear on our vision for the rebuild.

After that, I'm having a private meeting with the architect to go over the design for the building that's going to house our brand-new Hands-On Center. In conjunction with our petting farm, the Hands-On Center will coordinate with special needs facilities at local schools to bring in children with physical and mental disabilities to meet the animals. Albie, my cousin, is going to be in charge of this, but he's just left for a vacation to France with his girlfriend. After seeing the architect, I'm also meeting with Albie's stand-in to go over the IT schedule for the week to make sure he doesn't have any questions.

Lastly, I'm taking a conference call with the designers of a new Ark over in Hawke's Bay. And that's all before lunch.

All the meetings will take place at my house. Everyone's used to that. I'm fine all the time I can control the environment. It's only when I meet people outside of the house that I get into trouble.

I've been a little better since the cyclone. Fear for the staff and the animals forced me to join them in the Ark, and since then I've visited several times to check on the progress. I'm proud of myself for going out, even though I have to lie down for a while when I get back before I stop shaking.

Just the thought of it makes my heart start to race, so I take deep breaths and count the planks in the fence as I head back to the path leading up to the house.

I return just after ten, expecting to see my housekeeper's car gone because she only comes in for a couple of hours on a Monday, but to my surprise it's still there. I open the front door, standing back to let Willow and Spike in, and see Paula in the kitchen, hands clasped before her, apparently waiting for me.

"Hey." I hang my jacket on the peg by the door and unwind my scarf. "Everything okay?"

"Do you have a few minutes to talk?" she asks.

"Of course." I join her in the kitchen, switch on the coffee machine, then turn and lean against the worktop.

Paula is medium height, a little plump, and has gray hair cut short. She stands before me, twisting her hands. She comes in three mornings a week to clean, tidy, and cook for me. She's efficient and quiet, and keeps to herself, which suits me just fine. In the few conversations I've had with her, I've discovered she's fifty-five, married to Ken, has two daughters, and has an eighty-year-old mother in Auckland who's recently been diagnosed with bowel cancer.

"I told you my mother has been unwell…" she begins. "Well, she needs to have radiotherapy treatment, and that means staying at the hospital for six weeks. And after that she's going to need looking after for a while until she can get back on her feet."

"And you'd like to be there for her," I say. "Of course, that makes perfect sense."

Her cheeks flush. "Thank you for understanding."

"Family comes first, Paula. When are you going?"

"I thought maybe Wednesday. That gives me a day to get straight here."

"No worries at all. I'll contact the agency and get someone to cover for you until you get back."

"Well, actually… I know someone who might be suitable, if you're interested."

"Oh?"

"Yes, I have a friend who's looking for work. She's a lovely woman, smart, pleasant, funny… I think you'd like her."

"Would she be happy knowing it's only temporary work until you return?"

She nods. "She's actually a cake decorator and ran her own business in Hamilton, but she's recently moved up to the bay."

"She's transferring her business here?"

Paula hesitates. "Well, that's the thing…" She bites her bottom lip.

"Spit it out," I tell her good-naturedly.

"She's nearly eight months pregnant," she says. "She wants to wait until the baby's born before she gets stuck into the business again, but she's desperate for money." Her eyes meet mine. They hold nervousness and a touch of pity. "I won't be offended if you say no."

"Paula—"

"I shouldn't even have mentioned it, it's just that she's struggling a bit, and I promised I'd try to help, but I don't expect you to—"

"Of course she should come here," I say. "It's not a problem at all."

She blows out a long breath. "Are you sure? Please don't say yes just for me…"

"I like helping people," I tell her truthfully. "Are you sure it won't be too much for her?"

"A bit of vacuuming and tidying up? Mr. King, you keep your house impeccably clean and tidy. I feel embarrassed taking money from you sometimes."

I roll my eyes; I've never been able to get her to use my first name. "I hate dusting and ironing," I tell her. "You've been an absolute joy."

She blushes again. "Well, to be honest, I'd be relieved if Abigail—Abby—worked here. She told me the only job she could get was working in a stationery warehouse, and she'd have to carry boxes, and she'd be on her feet all day."

"Can she cook?" I ask. Paula bakes the occasional lasagna or moussaka for me and freezes them, so if I don't feel like cooking in the evening, I can just throw a portion in the microwave.

"I don't know how much ordinary cooking she does, but she's an amazing baker. She can make a hundred different types of muffins. And get her to bake you one of her sponge cakes—they're light as air."

"Sounds amazing," I say with a smile. "If she wants to start on Wednesday, she's very welcome."

"Thank you so much. It's going to mean the world to her. She's had a tough time, and… well, I'd better not say too much, but she'll be thrilled, I know she will."

I walk with her to the front door, where she slips on her coat and picks up her purse.

"Thank you," she says again.

"Best of luck with your mom," I tell her. "I hope it all goes well."

To my surprise, she lifts a hand and cups my cheek. "You're a good man, Noah King," she says softly. "I hope you find what you're looking for."

Then, seeming embarrassed at her gesture, she scurries out of the house to her car. With a brief wave, she gets in and heads out onto the main road.

I shut the door, go into the kitchen, and take the mug of coffee through to the living room. Walking up to the glass sliding doors, I open them to let the dogs out and stand in the doorway, looking out across the Pacific Ocean.

My stomach is a knot of emotions, and when I have a sip of coffee it takes immense effort to get my throat to relax enough to swallow it down.

She's nearly eight months pregnant...

Unbidden, my thoughts float up onto the wintry breeze, which carries them off into the past. Lisa had loved being pregnant. At eight months, she'd been the very spirit of joy. She'd painted the baby's bedroom in our old house yellow, and she'd stuck Pooh Bear decals all over the walls—pictures of Pooh with his honeypot, Tigger bouncing around, and Eeyore with his sad face. She'd bought a beautiful mobile to hang above the cot, and she'd hand-stitched a quilt in pinks and blues so it would fit the baby no matter if it was a boy or a girl.

It was a girl, but she never got to use it.

After Lisa died, I used to sit in the rocking chair she'd bought to nurse the baby, staring at the decals as the mobile turned around and around above the cot, playing *London Bridge is Falling Down*, thinking what a bizarre choice of song it was.

That was ten years ago. And I'm still fucked up. I don't think I'll ever be un-fucked, if that's a word. I'm forty-two now. No spring chicken, as my mother would say. And there are days when my agoraphobia is as bad as when it started.

I don't know why my grief takes this form. It's not depression, as such; I don't have black moods, and even though sometimes—like this morning—my thoughts wander to what it would be like to not feel this way anymore, I've never seriously considered ending my own life. I'm not angry. And I'm fine in my own home. All I know is that when I set foot outside, it takes the same effort as it would to move a mountain to get my body to look as if it's working normally—to walk, talk, and interact with people. And ninety-nine percent of the time, it's too much for me, and I have to turn around and go back.

People often think agoraphobia is a fear of going outdoors, but it's not. It's a type of anxiety disorder in which someone fears and avoids places or situations that make them feel trapped, helpless, or embarrassed. For me, it's just an overwhelming feeling of not being able to cope, and of letting those I love down. It's crippling, and I hate it, but I've had ten different counselors over the years, and none of them have been able to help me conquer it.

I don't have a fear of pregnant women, as such, although if I was forced to admit it, I'm relieved I don't have much contact with them. It's going to be a challenge to have this Abigail in my house, and awkward to have to find yet another housekeeper when it's time for her to give birth. But I want to help. But the last thing she would want, I'm sure, is me freaking out every time she lifts something heavier than the kettle, or panicking if she winces when the baby kicks.

I couldn't have said no to Paula any more than fly, though. The one thing in life that makes me feel better is helping people, and if I can help this woman, especially if she's had a tough time, whatever that means, then maybe it won't be such a bad thing.

Anyway, I suppose there are worse things than having a housekeeper who cooks a hundred different types of muffins.

There's change in the air; I can feel it. It makes me uneasy. I like my life the way it is. But I learned a long time ago that the worst thing you can do is try to fight it. So I close my eyes and surrender to the wintry breeze that blows across my face, tasting salt on my lips, and hope that whatever happens, it blows past me and leaves me standing rather than knocking me down and leaving me lying in its wake.

Chapter Two

Abigail

"I don't want you working," Tom says. "I've told you this a hundred times."

As calmly as I can, I pull on the one pair of stretchy maternity pants I own and settle them comfortably over my bump. "We need the money. I've got to do something."

He leans against the doorjamb, scowling at me. I choose one of my tunics, pull it over my head, and let it fall, relieved to be dressed. He's not one of those guys who finds pregnant women's bodies attractive, and I hate thinking he's looking at me with distaste.

"I don't see why you can't get started on the cakes," he says for the umpteenth time. "You said there's always a market for birthday and wedding cakes."

"There's no point me starting when I'm immediately going to have to take a couple of months off when the baby comes. It makes more sense to wait until I'm ready." The words come automatically; I've said them dozens of times before. I know he won't be listening.

I start applying some mascara in the mirror, gritting my teeth against the tears that glimmer in my eyes, as they seem to all the time. It's the baby, I think. But it's hard to lie to yourself. Baby hormones are only part of the reason I'm emotional. I can't help but think how different I'd be feeling right now if Tom would come up and give me a hug, stroke my bump, and tell me how beautiful I am, and how much he's looking forward to seeing his baby for the first time.

As I stroke the brush through my lashes, my mother's words come back to haunt me. *Find a man who'll smudge your lipstick, Abby, not your mascara.* I didn't listen. Who listens to their mother when they're eighteen?

I wonder whether she's surprised that Tom and I have been together for fourteen years. I guess she knows. We're so-called 'friends' on Facebook so she would have seen the photos I posted recently of our move up to the Bay of Islands. She never comments on them, though. Maybe she's changed her account. Maybe she's dead. Would someone inform me if that happened?

My thoughts are like confetti on the wind; it's hard to keep track of them. I'm constantly daydreaming, finding comfort in being in a fantasy world so different from my own. I have to drag myself back to the present.

"Who is this guy, anyway," Tom is saying. "I've heard he can't go out of the house. That's just fucking weird."

"He has agoraphobia." I dust powder over my face, then add a slick of lip gloss. "Paula says she hardly ever sees him."

It's not true. Paula told me she adores Noah King. She said he's quiet, gentle, funny, warm to his friends, that he works incredibly hard considering he doesn't leave the house, and he's very sad. She told me about what happened with his wife and baby, and said that's why he's now housebound, restrained and constrained by his grief. It must have been some marriage, I think, to cause a man to continue to grieve ten years after the death of his wife. I'm so envious it makes my stomach churn.

But I can't say any of this to Tom. Life with him has become a minefield. I need Princess Diana to come back from the afterlife and campaign to make it safer for me. One step off the road and everything blows up in my face. I could have handled it once, but now I'm conscious of the effect negative emotions might have on the baby, so I just turn away when he says something that makes me mad and go outside and dig the veggie patch.

We've got the best-dug veggie patch in the Northland at the moment. I wouldn't be surprised if I hit China, the amount of digging I've been doing.

He's not finished yet, though. "Keep your phone on you at all times. Call me if this bastard so much as smiles at you."

"I'll do nothing of the sort," I say heatedly, with a touch of my old spirit. "I wish you didn't believe the worst of everyone and everything. You drag me down. I was feeling happy when I got up this morning." I toss my lip gloss into my purse irritably.

"I'm just worried about you." Tom comes over to me then. "You walk along looking up at the stars, and you don't see the potholes in front of you."

"I'd rather do that than glue my gaze to the tarmac and never see the sky."

He looks down at me, but he makes no attempt to touch me. No hug, no kiss. I know I should make an effort to reach out to him. *You get back what you give out*, was another of my mother's epithets. But I can't bear to see him recoil, or to feel him stiffen when I slip my arms around him. I can't bear the rejection. And so I turn away, pick up my purse, and slip past him.

"What time will you be back?" he asks.

"Not sure," I reply, taking my jacket from the peg by the front door. Paula told me the hours are nine to twelve, Mondays, Wednesdays, and Fridays, so I could be home by twelve-thirty, but I feel a stubborn refusal to admit it. This afternoon I might go to the movies. Try to cheer myself up a bit. Although we can't really afford it. Maybe just go for a drive, then. Take in the beauty of the bay.

I leave the house and close the door behind me.

Ooh, it's chilly today. Winterless north, my ass. I get into the car, start it, and put the heater on, blowing onto my hands as it warms up. The vehicle rattles and bangs like a clown car. Jeez, I hope it hangs in there; the last thing we can afford is a new car. "I hope the summer here is as good as everyone says it is," I say to Peanut. That's the nickname I've given to the baby, because the first time I saw it on the scan, it looked like a peanut. I'll think of something a bit nicer for his or her real name.

I head out of town and take the turnoff to the Waitangi Treaty Grounds. I haven't been there yet. Tom's not interested in history, and you have to pay to get in, so it's a treat I'll have to save for when I've started up the business again and I have a little extra money.

I indicate at the turnoff for Noah's Ark and drive slowly up the road. Paula told me Noah's house lies beyond the Ark, and I can see the road curving around to a large house built high on a hill. It must have an amazing view of the bay.

I slow the car as I drive past the Ark. It's bigger than I thought. Paula said the cyclone damaged the corner of the building, and sure enough it's just a scatter of bricks, and I can see where they've sawn off the big tree that apparently crashed through the roof.

I stop the car by the entrance, leaving the engine running. The front of the main building is covered with a huge, colorful mural of different breeds of cats and dogs in an ark. The sign nearby says there's a veterinary clinic, a daycare facility, and a grooming center. There's also a petting farm to one side, and a cluster of office buildings. It's an impressive site. Paula said Noah is the brains behind the project, although he has several cousins who work there, too.

A woman of around my own age is approaching the gate to the car park next to the entrance, and she smiles at me, changing her direction to approach my car. I lower the window, embarrassed to be caught gawping.

"Are you okay?" she asks. "Can I help at all?" She's tall and slender, with long dark hair in a braid. She's wearing a sweatshirt with an SPCA badge, and underneath it are the words Animal Welfare Inspector. I like her already.

"I'm heading up to Mr. King's house," I tell her. "I just stopped for a moment to have a look at the Ark as I haven't been here before."

"Oh, you must be Abigail." She holds out her hand. "Noah said you were coming. I'm Izzy; I'm one of the vets at the center."

"Oh, hello." I shake her hand. "This place looks amazing. I'm so sorry to hear about the damage."

"Blessing in disguise," Izzy says. "We're redesigning. We really needed more rooms, and we're going to open a boarding kennels as well." She straightens as a man approaches from behind.

"Jesus, it's freezing out here." He shoves his hands in his pockets as he walks up to us. He's a big guy, tall, broad-shouldered, handsome, in a boy-next-door kind of way. "Hi." He smiles at me.

"This is Abigail," Izzy says. "Noah's new friend. Abigail, this is Hal."

I flush at her use of the word 'friend' as I shake hands with Hal. "Abby, please. And I'm his housekeeper," I correct. "I haven't even met him yet."

"Oh, you'll be friends," Hal says. "Noah gets on with everyone." He smiles again, warming me through on this cold day.

"If you want to have a look around the Ark, I'd be happy to show you sometime," Izzy says. "Most days when I'm not on call I'm free at lunch around one."

"Thank you, I might take you up on that." I haven't made any friends since moving to the bay, and her generosity touches me. My throat tightens—baby hormones again.

"I'd better go," I say, my voice a little husky. "Don't want to be late on my first day."

Hal grins. "Just carry along this road and it'll take you straight there."

"Thank you."

"Bye." Izzy waves, and the two of them start walking back to the Ark. He puts his arms around her shoulders, and she slips a hand into the back pocket of his jeans. It's a familiar gesture you wouldn't make with a colleague, so they're obviously an item. For the first few years, there's a need to constantly touch each other, to mark out your territory, to prove your love. Tom and I used to do things like that.

I put the car into drive and head down the road to the house at the end.

I pull up out the front and turn off the engine. The house is huge. Feeling as if I'm playing a role in a New Zealand version of *Downton Abbey*, I get out of the car and approach the front door. I've never cleaned for anyone before. Tom says it's demeaning doing someone else's dirty washing and scrubbing their floors, but it's good, honest work, and I'd rather do it than move boxes in a warehouse.

As I reach the front door, it opens. And this must be Noah. He smiles as I walk up to him. He's moderately tall, maybe six foot, a little shorter and slenderer than Hal. He doesn't look anything like him, really. He has gray hair, so he must be older, maybe forty or so, and lines at the corners of his eyes. He's gorgeous, though, and his smile is warm. That's a surprise. I was expecting someone weasel-like and nervous, cowering behind the door.

"You must be Abigail," he says, stepping back to let me in, and holding out a hand. "I'm Noah."

"Hello." I slip my hand into his, and his warm fingers close around mine in a strong grip. His eyes meet mine briefly. His are an attractive violet blue, like the sky, late on a summer evening.

He closes the door behind me and releases my hand. "Can I take your jacket?"

"Oh, thank you." I unzip it, surprised when he moves behind me to take it from me as it slides down my arms. A gentlemanly maneuver.

Tom's never done anything like that in all the years we've been together.

He hangs it on the peg by the door and gestures for me to precede him into the house. I walk forward, forgetting everything as I take in the magnificent room in front of me. It's all open-plan, the entrance hall leading to a large kitchen on my left, and down a slope to the living room beyond. It's huge, with a high ceiling that makes it feel a bit like a cathedral. The whole of the front wall is glass, looking out onto a deck that stretches the length of the house. To the left is an octagonal conservatory housing two German Shepherds; I can see their noses pressed up against the glass, watching me.

I walk across the living room and up to the windows, my jaw dropping at the sight of the Bay of Islands spread out before me. It's truly magnificent.

"Not a bad view," Noah says, joining me by the window. I look up at him; he's smiling.

"It's amazing," I tell him. "Can you get down to the beach from here?"

"Yes, there's a pathway over there." He points to a gate in the fence that runs around the garden. "It goes all the way down to the beach. I take the dogs there most mornings. They love the walk."

I'm surprised for the third time in as many minutes. I thought he didn't go out of the house at all.

"It's a beautiful house," I tell him, somewhat wistfully. I can't imagine ever having the kind of money that would enable me to live somewhere like this. We rent a very small one-bedroomed cottage. We've been late on the fortnightly rent twice since we moved there four months ago, and we're going to be late this time too.

But there's no point in worrying about it. Worry doesn't pay the bills. Hopefully Noah will pay me for today's work, and with this and Friday's cleaning, and the little I have put aside, I should have enough to pay the rent.

One thing at a time, I tell myself. It's how I live now. Day to day. Minute to minute, almost. There's no point in looking too far ahead.

It only makes me sad.

Chapter Three

Noah

Abigail's lost in thought, staring out of the window, although I don't think she's seeing the view.

She's not at all what I expected. Paula said Abigail is her friend, and so I'd expected her to be older, maybe late thirties or early forties, pregnant with her third or fourth child. But she looks Izzy's age, around thirty, with long glossy chestnut-brown hair pulled back into a ponytail. She's wearing soft black pants and a blue T-shirt over the top. Her bump pushes the fabric out, but she's actually quite thin, lacking the extra pregnancy weight most women seem to gain.

She has dark shadows under her eyes, and I'm reminded once again of Paula's comments, "she's desperate for money," "she's struggling a bit," and "she's had a tough time." I'm startled by the thought that she might not be eating enough. She looks sad, not at all how a pregnant woman excited about the birth of her baby should look.

Despite this, there's something beautiful and elegant about her. She's like an exquisite painting, the Girl with a Pearl Earring, all pale skin and big brown eyes.

Her gaze comes back to me now, and she blinks a couple of times as if she's remembering where she is. "Sorry," she says, "I zoned out for a minute. I keep doing that lately."

"They say every child you have destroys a quarter of your brain," I tell her, wanting to see what she looks like when she smiles.

Her lips curve up a little. "I struggle enough with a whole working brain, let alone three-quarters of one."

So it's her first child. I push away the memories of Lisa hovering in the corner of my mind and gesture with my head for her to follow me across the room. "So, do you prefer Abigail or Abby?"

"Abby's fine," she says.

"Okay. Let me show you around and tell you what Paula liked to do. It's up to you then. Anything you can manage will be great." I don't want to patronize her, but equally I don't want her thinking she has to work her fingers to the bone to earn her money.

She gives me a strange look. "You're the boss. I'll do whatever you need."

"If you have that sort of mentality we're going to get along fine."

She gives a little laugh, the tension disappearing from her shoulders. Wow, she's really quite beautiful.

"Shall I call you Mr. King?" she asks, a little shyly.

"Oh God, don't start, you're as bad as Paula. It's Noah. Come this way."

I lead her into the large dining room that stretches the width of the house. It has a long wooden table that seats twelve, with a central section that can be lifted out to expand it to seat sixteen.

"Wow," she says. "Do you entertain a lot?"

"Occasionally."

"Do you do the cooking?" She wanders over to the window that overlooks the valley.

"Sometimes," I admit. "I have to be in the mood."

"Paula said she prepares you dinners."

"Yes, she's been very good to me. She was worried I wasn't eating enough. I tend to forget when I'm working."

She turns and surveys me. Her gaze slips down me like a silk scarf, sending a shiver down my spine. "You are a little on the thin side."

"You can talk," I tease. "You're supposed to be eating for two."

"Rent comes before food," she says brightly, as if it's a joke. I don't laugh, though, so she turns and walks through to the kitchen.

So I was right—it's a money issue. I wait a moment, and then I follow her.

"This is a beautiful kitchen," she says, running her fingertips over the equipment. "Oh, what an amazing food processor."

It's a top-of-the-range Sunbeam, with every shredding, grating, and slicing blade you could ever need.

"I understand you're a baker," I say, not wanting to admit the processor cost seven hundred dollars.

"Yes. I had a cake-decorating business down in Hamilton."

"You've moved up here recently?"

"Four months ago." She opens a drawer and checks out the utensils. "We're having a fresh start." She speaks without enthusiasm.

So she has a partner, then. And they've had problems. Are continuing to, by the almost indistinguishable touch of sarcasm in her voice.

"Come this way," I say softly.

I lead her across the kitchen and entrance hallway to the other part of the house. On the right is my office—an airy room with lots of light. My desk sits by the window, and there's another table covered in plans for the rebuilding of the Ark. A couple of filing cabinets stand against the wall. That's about it. I like space.

"This is where the magic happens?" she asks with a smile. "I heard you were the brains behind the Ark."

"I was the initial spark. The light bulb, if you like. Everyone else did all the work." I lead her out and across the hallway to the gym.

"Jesus." She stops in the doorway and stares. "Are you training for the Olympics or something?"

I look at the various pieces of equipment, the weights, the treadmill. "I don't go out of the house," I point out. "It's important to get some sort of exercise."

She lifts her gaze to me then. We're standing quite close together, in the doorway, and I can see every detail of her face. Her skin is flawless, pale and smooth, apart from a scar, probably from chickenpox, on her chin. She also has a small mole on her right cheekbone. Her eyes are dark brown around the pupil, but light brown, like warm caramel, around the edge of the iris. She has long girly lashes.

"You said you walk the dogs," she whispers.

"That's true. But it's more of a meander. Spike can't go that fast on the sand. He's in a wheelchair."

Her eyebrows rise. "Your dog?"

"Yeah, he was in a car accident and damaged his spine. I had a wheelchair made for him. He's fine now, but sometimes his wheels get stuck in the sand." I smile.

She blinks a few times as if she has no idea what to make of me. "Paula said you have agoraphobia."

"Yes."

"Do you mind talking about it?"

I look at the floor for a moment. I'm not used to discussing it with other people. I've accepted who I am and that it's not going to go away, and I've learned to live with it. Occasionally, I'll get a gentle prod from Leon, my brother, or one of my cousins, to come to dinner, because they feel as if they should ask every few months, but otherwise, my friends and family don't mention it. If I'm organizing meetings, such as the one with the architect, I tell them I'd rather it be at my house, and they rarely ask why. Sometimes I think it's because Leon or one of the others has quietly told them, at other times it's because people are rarely interested in anything but themselves. So it's unusual for someone to ask me about it outright.

"No, I don't mind," I reply, lifting my gaze to hers. It's only fair, if she's coming to work here. I can imagine how strange it must seem to other people.

She nibbles her bottom lip. "You don't go out at all, apart from the beach?"

"I went to the Ark a couple of times after the cyclone to check on the building progress, but I haven't been this week." I have tried. I've stepped outside a couple of times, but each time my heart begins to race, and I've ended up going back indoors.

Her gaze is gentle as it brushes over my face. "How does it make you feel if you go outside?"

"Panicky." It's a broad term. It ranges from mild anxiety to full-blown fear. I try not to let myself get to that stage.

"Do you worry that something is going to happen?"

I slide my hands into my pockets. "Not consciously. Subconsciously… maybe. It's gone way past any rational thought. I just associate being outside with feeling fear. But it's okay. I'm happy here. I have no burning ambition to change now."

"What about if you need to see a doctor or something?"

"I pay for them to visit me."

"It helps to have money," she says.

"It does. I appreciate it. We didn't have money when we were young."

"You're not from a rich family?"

"No, not at all. My mother married my stepfather when I was thirteen. You might have heard of him—Matt King. The author of the Ward Seven stories."

Her jaw drops. "Of course I've heard of him. I've bought several of his books to read to Peanut when he's born."

My lips curve up. "Peanut?"

She gives a short laugh and strokes her bump. "It's what I call him. Or her. Tom didn't want to know the sex." She turns away and continues walking slowly along the corridor. I fall into step beside her. She doesn't like talking about her husband. I glance at her left hand; she's not wearing a ring.

She stops by the next room. "My bedroom," I tell her as we stand in the doorway. It's a large room, spacious, with little furniture. The bed faces the window and has an amazing view of the Pacific. There's a bathroom off to the side, with a spacious bath, although I tend to use the shower more.

She gives me a quick smile and continues on. There are several spare bedrooms at this end of the house. Leon, Hal, and Albie, used to stay here sometimes in the early days, if we'd had a few drinks and they couldn't be bothered to drive home. Occasionally, if I have a dinner party, someone will stop over. The rooms are all pleasant and light.

She looks in the doors and moves on. "So what happened after your mom met Matt King? Did you live with them?"

"Yes. I was… a bit of a troublemaker back then. I know it's hard to believe." I give her a grin. "But Matt was a great father. When he realized I was interested in art, he encouraged me to go to art school. I ended up painting murals."

"You painted the one on the front of the Ark?"

"Yes."

"Wow, that was terrific—you really have talent."

"I've won awards," I say as modestly as I can, conscious that I want to impress this woman. I don't want her to think of me as a weak guy, overshadowed by my affliction. I'm more than that. It doesn't define me. "I painted other murals inside the buildings, too."

"That's amazing," she says, and warmth spreads through me at her genuine admiration. "Matt must be so proud of you."

"Yeah, they both are."

"What about your birth father?" She moves further along the corridor. "Where does he live?"

"He died."

She stops and turns to me. "Oh, I'm so sorry, putting my foot in it as usual."

"Not at all. He…" I clear my throat. "He took his own life."

Her brows draw together. "Oh, Noah, you've had some terrible losses. I'm not surprised you feel as if it's you against the world."

That's exactly how I feel, and it's the first time anyone's ever expressed it like that. My surprise must show in my face, because she gives a small smile before she stops and stares at the next room. "Oh!" She walks into it. "Oh my God, what an amazing room."

It's a big room with three walls lined with shelves of books. The fourth wall looks out across the fields, with the Ark in the distance. There's a sofa and armchairs, a desk against the wall with a computer, a table with a coffee machine, and a mini fridge with cans of soda and bottles of beer. "I spend a lot of time here," I tell her.

"I didn't think anyone had libraries anymore." She walks around the room, looking at the books, occasionally taking one out to leaf through it before returning it to the shelf.

I lean against the doorjamb and watch her. It's nice to see someone else enjoying the room. I love it in here. I'd say it's my favorite room in the house, but I do adore the conservatory that looks over the sea, and the kitchen when I'm cooking with music playing in the background, and the gym when I'm in the mood to work out.

Her hand strays subconsciously to her bump as she tips her head to the side to look at the titles of the books. She strokes it lightly, her fingers brushing across the surface of the tunic. I wonder whether she touches her partner like that—tender, affectionate. I haven't been touched like that for ten years, unless you count the occasional hug I've had from my mother, Izzy, or the other girls at the Ark.

I've missed it. The thought surprises me. I've trained myself not to think about it. Not to dwell on the way Lisa would lie beside me in bed, trailing her fingers across my chest and belly while we watched the TV. How her hand would slip into mine while we walked, partly because she liked to be close to me, partly as a show of possession to other women: *Watch out girls, he's mine.* I haven't belonged to someone for a long, long time. There's freedom in that, but also a sense of deep loss. It's nice, to feel loved and wanted.

"I'm not surprised you never leave the house," Abby says. "I wouldn't either, if I lived somewhere like this."

Her compliment makes me smile. I'm glad she likes it.

She leaves the books reluctantly and walks back to me. "Did you build the house yourself?"

"Well, not with my own hands. I don't know one end of a plank of wood from the other. But yes, I had it designed. If I was going to be housebound, it had to be somewhere I felt comfortable in."

I show her my conference room, where I hold meetings with people from the Ark as well as visitors. Then, together, we walk back through the house to the living room.

"That's the conservatory," I tell her, gesturing to where the dogs are watching us, their noses pressed against the glass. "And that's Spike and Willow."

"Can I meet them?"

"Of course, if you're sure." German Shepherds are big dogs, and a lot of people are wary of them.

"You're surprised," she says with amusement.

"Kinda. Paula preferred them to stay in the conservatory while she cleaned."

"Really? Wow. Well, you don't have to lock them up on my account. I love dogs. I'd have one myself but…" Her voice trailed off, but I knew what she was going to say. *But Tom doesn't like them.*

I've never met the guy, and I already dislike him intensely.

"Come on." I lead her over to the conservatory. "They're reasonably well trained and shouldn't jump up." When she nods, I open the door and say to them firmly, "Come and say hello to Abby. Gently, now, you two. Gently." I hold out a hand, palm down, indicating they mustn't jump up. If they show any signs of being overexcited, I'll lock them back in the room.

But they behave impeccably, coming up to Abby with wagging tails, thrilled when she drops to her knees and holds out her hands for them to sniff before scratching behind their ears. Within minutes, Spike's looking at her as if she's a rare steak, and Willow's on her back with her feet in the air.

I kinda know how they feel.

Chapter Four

Abigail

After fussing the dogs, I try to get to my feet, but it's a struggle, and in the end Noah holds out a hand and helps me up. "Sorry," I tell him, brushing my tunic down, a little breathless from being in such close contact with him. "My center of gravity is a bit off. I feel like an upturned turtle half the time."

"If it's any consolation, you don't look it." He smiles as we head back into the living room. He's probably just being polite, but his compliment warms me through.

"So… I've not exactly done anything like housekeeping before," I admit. "Are you certain you're happy to take me on?"

"I'm sure you'll be extremely capable," he replies.

"Okay… um, thanks. To be honest, the place is pretty spotless. What do you want me to do, exactly?" His house is tidier and cleaner than mine.

"Anything that I don't have to do is a bonus," he admits. "A brief dust, a quick vacuum, a tidy up."

"Washing?"

"I do my own laundry. How are you at ironing shirts, though? 'Cause that's one of my pet hates."

I chuckle. "I'm happy to do that."

"Cool. And cooking. If you can rustle up the occasional meal, that would be great. You're welcome to use anything in the pantry, fridge, or freezer."

"Okay." That makes me happy. "Do you like muffins?"

"I adore muffins. Paula said you know a hundred different types. I'm happy for you to work your way through your recipe list."

I laugh. "Noted."

"How do you know Paula?" he asks me curiously. "Are you related?"

"No. We met at a self-help group." I walk away, into the kitchen, and open the cupboard under the sink. "Well, I'd better get started. I've already wasted half an hour looking around."

"All right. I'll be in my office if you need anything—don't hesitate to ask."

"I will. Thanks." I glance at him as he walks away, Spike at his side. Noah fascinates me. His eyes are watchful but kind. His house is amazing. He obviously has enough money to buy anything he wants. And yet he has this really strange affliction. I can't imagine not being able to leave the house. It would make me claustrophobic. And yet, would I feel the same if I lived here? With all this space, this beautiful view?

He also smells really nice. I like guys who smell nice. Tom's allergic to something in most men's fragrances so he wouldn't use them even if we could afford them. It's not his fault, but there's something wonderful about a man who uses aftershave.

Noah disappears down the corridor, and I drop my gaze to Willow, who's more interested in staying to see what I get up to. After giving her a quick fuss, I have a look at the cleaning stuff under the sink, select a cloth and some polish, and get to work.

As I suspected, there's not a lot of dust around, so I take time to orient myself as I move through the rooms, checking dust traps, running my finger over the top of doorways, and looking beneath furniture. Paula is a thorough cleaner, thank goodness, so all I have to do is flick the duster around, and then I get out the vacuum and pick up the few bits on the carpet that the dogs have brought in.

I pass Noah working in his study, pull his door to so I don't disturb him too much, and vacuum the rest of the house, tidying as I go, putting away magazines and books, emptying trash cans, straightening picture frames. I'm done in an hour. There's no ironing in the laundry room, so I go into the kitchen.

I spend a pleasant ten minutes looking in the cupboards, the fridge and freezer, and the pantry. He's obviously a cook himself, as there's every herb and spice a chef could ever want, and expensive cuts of meat in the freezer. I decide to make something simple to begin with, so I find some minced lamb in the fridge and settle on a shepherd's pie.

I chop and fry an onion and some carrots with the mince, add some garlic and fresh thyme, some stock, tomato puree, and Worcestershire sauce, and let it cook for a while before spreading it across the bottom of six individual white dishes. I boil and mash some potatoes with butter and milk, and spoon those over the top. Then I place them in the oven.

I wash up, and then I get out the ingredients for some banana muffins.

As I sift the flour with the baking powder and baking soda, I realize I feel happy for the first time in weeks, if not months. The sunlight is streaming through the windows, falling across the living room in squares like pats of butter. It must cost a fortune to heat the place with the high ceilings, but the heat from the huge gas fire set into the wall fills the room with warmth.

I muse on how lovely it must be not to have to worry about turning off a fire when you leave a room as I mash the bananas and combine them with sugar, egg, and melted butter. Money has become my whole life. I guess it's the same with most people, I think, as I stir in the sifted flour. In fact I'm luckier than most—I have a roof over my head, a partner, I'm pregnant, and I live in the Bay of Islands, which features on many people's bucket lists.

My hand slows, the spoon gliding through the mixture, and my gaze drifts up and away to the Pacific Ocean. I have been blessed with a child, which is more than many women have, but apart from that, I don't feel lucky.

Still, there's not much I can do about it now. I bring my gaze back to the muffin tins I found in one of the cupboards, fit some paper cases in, and pour in the mixture. Then I take out the shepherd's pies, place the muffins in, and set the timer.

I'm tempted to lick the wooden spoon, but it contains raw egg, so I know I mustn't.

While they cook, I clean up, washing up all the bowls and measuring devices and placing them where I found them. By the time I've finished, the room is filled with the smell of baking, and it's obviously strong enough to draw Noah out of his office, because he comes wandering in with a smile, sniffing the air.

"Wow, something smells amazing."

"They're just about to come out." I open the oven and pull out the tray, pleased to see them all lightly browned, and place it on the heat-resistant pad on the worktop. "Banana muffins today."

"Fantastic."

"And shepherd's pie for tonight." I gesture at the dishes sitting to one side. "I'll freeze the rest when they're cool."

"They look amazing. Thank you, Abby."

"You're welcome." I turn away to hide a blush. "I'll give the muffins a couple of minutes and then take them out the pans, and you can have one if you like."

"Will you join me? We could have a cup of coffee in the conservatory. Or tea, if you'd rather. I've plenty of herbal varieties."

I hesitate, knowing I shouldn't. But the muffins smell amazing, and I've been on my feet for a couple of hours now, and I don't want my ankles to swell.

"Are you sure?" I ask. "Aren't you busy?"

"I've got thirty minutes before I have to take a conference call. Plenty of time for a cuppa."

The thought of a muffin is too tempting. "Okay, then."

"I'll make the drinks," he says. "What would you like?"

I choose green tea, and he makes himself a coffee while I ease the muffins out of the pan onto a cooling rack and put two on a plate. When we're ready, we take everything through to the conservatory.

There are four wicker chairs here filled with comfortable cushions. I lower myself carefully into one, and Noah sits beside me. The dogs, obviously well trained, don't ask for food, and instead Spike lies by Noah's feet, while Willow flops onto her side in the sunshine.

I sip my tea, then break apart the muffin, releasing a wisp of steam into the air. Oh God, it smells amazing. I place a piece in my mouth and chew it slowly, my eyes closed. Peanut does a sudden flip in my stomach, clearly excited at the thought of food.

I open my eyes to find Noah watching me over the rim of his coffee cup. I wonder if he's going to comment on my obvious pleasure, but he just smiles and says, "These are excellent," as he takes a bite of the muffin.

"I'm glad you like them."

"Your own recipe?"

"Oh, it's just a basic one, as I wanted to test out the oven. Some ovens cook quicker than others. Yours was just right, though."

"Paula said I have to get you to bake me one of your cakes. She said they're amazing."

I laugh. "I made one for our group and put fondant flowers all over it. It only took me half an hour, but they talked about it for weeks."

I wonder whether he's going to ask me what kind of help I need, but he doesn't. His eyes are watchful, but all he says is, "So tell me, how did you get into cake decorating?"

I could talk about baking until the cows come home, so I explain how I used to cook with my grandmother back in England, making all kinds of cakes and cookies in her big kitchen in Devon.

"How long have you been in New Zealand?" he asks. "You still have a British accent."

"Fourteen years," I tell him. "My partner, Tom, is a Kiwi. We met in London, and he persuaded me to come back with him. My mom was very upset. We never got on at the best of times, but when I announced I was leaving, she practically disowned me."

Noah's brow furrows. "That must have been difficult for you."

"It was. Still is."

"She didn't want you to move so far away?"

"That's part of the reason. It is a long way. I didn't care at the time, but of course I didn't factor in how much it was going to cost to fly back to see her. I haven't been able to afford to go back, and she doesn't want to come here, so…" My voice trails off.

"What was the other part of the reason?"

I sip my tea. "She disapproved of Tom. She thought he would be a bad influence on me."

I wait for him to ask if she was right, or why she thought that, but he doesn't. He takes another bite of muffin, then looks out of the window for a while, obviously thinking.

"Is your dad still alive?" he asks eventually, bringing his gaze back to me.

"Yes." I don't want to talk about my father. "Do you have any brothers and sisters?" I ask him.

He doesn't push the point. "One brother, Leon, and one sister, Clio. They're my half-brother and half-sister, technically. Same mother. I'm not related by blood to the Kings—the family who help me run the Ark, but we all call ourselves cousins. Nobody really cares. We all look out for each other here. The Ark is a sanctuary, after all." He smiles.

I wonder what it must be like to be surrounded by people who care about you. I feel so alone at the moment. I think of how friendly Izzy and Hal were, and how it would be to work somewhere like the Ark all the time. To have someone to celebrate with when things go right. To have support if things go wrong.

Noah finishes off his coffee. "Anyway, I'd better get ready for my call."

"Of course." I have the last mouthful of tea, and we take our plates and mugs back into the kitchen.

"I'll put these in the freezer," I tell him, gesturing at the shepherd's pies. "Do you want me to leave one out for you for tonight?"

"Yes, please. But actually, I was thinking, I doubt I'll get through six of those." He slides his hands into his pockets. "Would you like to take a couple home? And some of those muffins?" He's smiling, but his eyes are astute. He's seen through me.

How? What did I say that made him suspect? I'm not sure, but I'm embarrassed. "I couldn't," I stutter.

"They'll only go to waste," he says easily. "Unless it's too difficult for you." Again, his tone is gentle but his eyes are sharp. He suspects Tom is going to have a problem with it.

I look at the dishes. Tom will hate the charity, but I might be able to spin it as having made too much. They're going to taste amazing, and I'm sick of eating noodles and rice.

I swallow hard. "Well, if you're sure. I wouldn't want to make you fat."

He laughs. "I'll have to run an extra few hundred miles if I eat all those muffins." He goes over to a drawer and takes out a reusable supermarket bag, then covers two of the white dishes with lids before placing them inside. Then he finds a plastic box with a lid and puts four of the muffins in there before placing those in the bag, too.

"Let's get your coat," he says eventually. I follow him over to the front door, and he takes my jacket down and holds it up for me to slide my arms into. Finally, he hands me the bag.

"Thank you," I whisper, too full of emotion to say anything else.

"Thank you. I'm looking forward to dinner tonight. Oh, and of course, payment. Do you have your bank details? I'll transfer the money over."

I hesitate. If the money goes into our bank account, there's a danger it won't be there when the rent is due on Friday.

"Or I can give you cash," he says swiftly.

"If that's possible, that would be great."

"Give me a sec." He strides off around the corner, presumably to his office, then returns in less than a minute. He holds out the notes.

I take them. It's three times more than I was expecting. I look up at him, opening my mouth to query it.

"For today and an advance on Friday," he says. "With a bonus for making that amazing food." Again, he's guessed that I probably need it for rent.

My bottom lip trembles. I take a deep, shuddering breath. "Thank you," I whisper.

"I'll see you Friday?"

I nod, and he smiles. "Take care of yourself."

"You too." I walk to my car, knowing he's watching me.

The Ark is a sanctuary, after all.

For the first time in a long time, I feel a brief flicker of hope that I might make some real friends here. That I might not be alone when the baby comes.

The thought is enough to bring a smile to my lips, and I'm still smiling as I drive away.

Chapter Five

Noah

On Friday, I get back from my walk earlier than usual. I have a lot of work to do, and I want to be there when Abby turns up. I want to check that I didn't make things awkward for her by giving her the food on Wednesday. I saw her hesitation, and I knew she was thinking her partner wouldn't approve. I hope he didn't give her a hard time.

She turns up at five to nine in her old and battered red Toyota, and parks to one side, the same as last time, as if she's embarrassed to let me see it. I open the door as she approaches, and smile as she walks in. "Good morning."

"Good morning," I respond. Her returning smile is bright. I'm relieved she doesn't look worried.

"How are you today?" she asks.

"Good thanks." I close the door behind her, take her jacket as she slips it off, and hang it on the peg. "You?"

"I'm well, thank you."

"And Peanut?"

She laughs and strokes her bump. "He's good, too. Very active this morning. I think he's excited to be here." She walks through to the kitchen, places the bag she's carrying on the worktop, and takes out the white dishes and the plastic box that had held the food she'd taken home.

"The shepherd's pie was amazing," I tell her, standing beside her and resting a hip against the worktop. "Did you enjoy it?"

She gives me a wry glance. "You're quite the diplomat, aren't you?"

"Am I?"

She nudges me. "The pie was lovely, and so were the muffins. Thank you for your generosity."

"Jeez, you took the time and effort to make them."

"For which I got paid extremely well."

I shrug. "What's on the menu today?"

"I thought maybe a lasagna?"

"Mm. Terrific." I check my watch. "I have to go; I'm supposed to be making a phone call at nine."

"Okay. Anything special you want done today?"

"There are a few shirts to iron in the laundry room."

She grins. "I'll get started right away."

I leave her to it, pleased she seems a bit happier, and go into my office.

After the call to the council in Hawke's Bay, chasing up the resource consent application for the new Ark, I spend an hour or so going over the budgets that Leon wants to discuss with me later, making notes and jotting down a few questions. Then I pick up my iPad and take it through to the library.

In the distance, I can hear Abby in the kitchen, singing. I stop and listen, unused to the sound of a female voice in my house. Paula never sang; she was like a ghost around the place. Izzy and some of the other girls visit, of course, but this is different.

It's an old hymn, one I remember my mother singing to me as a child, 'I Danced in the Morning.' Or is it called 'Lord of the Dance'? I remember reading an article on the author of the song, Sydney Carter. He was inspired not only by his feelings about Jesus, but also by a statue of the Hindu God Shiva as Nataraja—the cosmic ecstatic dancer, and it was a tribute to Shaker music. Abby's voice is high and somewhat ethereal; I imagine the notes drifting up to the high ceiling, dancing on the sunlit beams.

Glad she seems happier, I go into the library, sit in an armchair with my feet up, and start reading through the departmental reports.

Most of them are short and to the point. Stefan talks about the new rooms we're having built for the veterinary center and suggests that once Clio—my sister—has qualified as a vet, she has one of the new rooms, because she won't be joining the Animal Welfare Team yet. "She's young," Stefan says, "and I think a couple of years in the center will benefit her before she thinks about joining the AWT." I smile; he's being diplomatic. Clio's a softie, and we both know she'd struggle to deal with belligerent owners refusing to give up their mistreated pets.

I read through Poppy's rundown of life at the petting farm. She's much more vocal on paper than she is face-to-face; like Albie, she struggles somewhat with communication, and is more able to voice her opinions when she has time to compose her thoughts. She used to be a primary school teacher, and she talks about how she can see the farm working with the new Hands-On unit and lists a few ideas of ways to get children with disabilities to have contact with the animals in a safe environment.

Jules's report on the grooming center is brisk and businesslike; she's run off her feet while Remy's away. Fitz's is the same, but then he's always like that. His army background means everything in Fitz's world is in order and runs on time.

Ryan's summary is longer; he gives a brief report on the rehoming center, then talks for a while about the app he developed, PetForever. People who are interested in rehoming a rescue animal can browse through the photos and descriptions of those available, and then book an appointment with Ryan on his online calendar, to ensure there aren't hordes of people traipsing around the center. My eyebrows rise as he tells me he's been approached by the Ministry for Children, who have been impressed by the app and are thinking of asking him to adapt it for their adoption agency.

"Of course it would only be for the initial stages of contact," he explains, "a way for those applying to record their backgrounds, social status, that kind of thing, and to calculate initial matches with pregnant women considering giving up their baby for adoption. Once their expression of interest is registered, social workers would carry out visits as normal and everything else would be done face-to-face, but it would be a way to begin the process and log applications without worrying about losing paper questionnaires." He sounds excited about the prospect. I'm pleased for him. He's had a tough time and deserves a break.

Hal's report always reads more like a diary. "The Animal Welfare Team rescued a total of sixteen animals," Hal states. "Izzy fell in love with a Beagle with eyes like Puss in Boots from *Shrek*. So it looks as if we're adopting another dog. Miss Daisy's like a mother with a newborn, fussing around it."

I smile as he names the rescue dog he adopted back in February. The Border Collie dotes on him, but then most animals do. He has a special charisma that makes every female within ten feet fall in love with him. It certainly worked with Izzy. Once he came to his senses and acknowledged his feelings for her, the poor girl didn't stand a chance.

I know Leon's not keen on relationships in the workplace, but I like that my cousins are finding love at the Ark. Hal and Izzy are getting married in September. Leon himself has Nix now, and they're planning on an early December wedding. And I'm pretty sure Albie and Remy will return from Paris engaged, because he's head over heels for her. I'm hopeful the others will eventually find their perfect match and find happiness.

Will the Ark work its magic on Abby, too?

I put down my iPad, get to my feet, and wander out into the kitchen. Some amazing smells are wafting through the house. The finished lasagna rests on the worktop, cooling in the six white dishes; she's now washing up the utensils from another batch of muffins, judging by the aroma that reaches my nostrils.

"Hey." She looks up and smiles as I approach. Her face is flushed from the heat of the oven. Her hands sparkle with soap suds. "How's the work going?"

"Good. I'm about done. They smell amazing. Is it coffee time?"

She laughs. "They'll be out in about five minutes. Perfect timing. Are you sure you're not too busy?"

"I don't have much on this afternoon. And anyway, I'm never too busy for a muffin."

"Fair enough."

I make the drinks as she finishes the dishes, and by the time she brings the muffins out, we're ready to go. She places two on plates, and we carry them through to the conservatory.

"This is beginning to be a habit," she says, curling up on one of the chairs and placing the plate with the muffin on her bump.

"I can think of worse habits to have." I smile and break my muffin open, releasing a spiral of steam.

We sip our drinks and eat our muffins in silence for a while. It's not an awkward silence; I get the feeling she's enjoying the moment as much as I am, a kind of shared peace.

"I heard you singing," I say eventually. "My mom used to sing that to me when I was young."

"Oh, sorry, did I disturb you?"

"Not at all. You have a lovely voice."

A touch of color appears on her cheekbones. I get the feeling she's not used to receiving compliments.

"So what do you have planned for the rest of the day?" I ask.

She pops a piece of muffin in her mouth and chews thoughtfully. "I'm supposed to be going to my group, but I don't know if I'll bother. Paula's not there, and with her gone... I'm not sure how helpful it is."

I sip my coffee. If she didn't want to talk about it, I'm sure she wouldn't have brought it up. I opt for humor, as usual. "I'd ask if it's a prenatal group, but I don't think Paula would be going to one of those."

She chuckles. "I think she'd be horrified at the thought. No. It's a group for people... whose partners are..." She lowers her gaze to her mug. "Gamblers."

It all clicks into place. Her partner has a gambling addiction. That's why they're short of money. And presumably why they've moved recently; he must have got into trouble wherever they were living before. *We're having a fresh start*, she'd said last time she was here. Clearly, it's not going swimmingly.

"Paula's husband is a gambler?" I asked, surprised I didn't know. But then why would I? It's hardly something that would come up in conversation.

Abby nods. "Being with her gives me hope. She's been married thirty years, and she's managed to get through it. She does have a large family to help her, though."

"Of course, your family is in England, isn't it? You don't have anyone here?"

"Not really. We've moved around a lot. If I have made friends, I've had to leave them behind when I've moved."

So she's completely alone. No wonder she seems so forlorn. I can only imagine how it must feel to be pregnant and living with a guy who gambles away your rent money, and you've nobody to help you.

"Tell me about your cake decorating business," I say.

As I'd hoped, she brightens a little. "It was called The Mad Batter."

I laugh. "That's brilliant."

"I thought so. I've always enjoyed baking, but I started to get into decorating and really enjoyed it. I made a birthday cake for a friend's son with a Spider-Man on the top, and other moms who were at the party thought it was brilliant. Soon I was getting requests left, right, and center. So I decided to set up a business from home. I had to apply for licenses and make business cards. It was a tough process but I really enjoyed it. I was just starting to make a name for myself." She drops her gaze to her mug.

"What happened?" I ask softly.

She uncurls her legs and stretches them out. She strokes her bump, subconsciously, I think, because she's lost in thought.

"Tom was a banker," she says. "He worked in investment, in stocks and shares. He'd go to work in the morning and come home at night, and he'd try to tell me about his day, but I'm not great at math, so even though I tried to understand what he was saying, it went over my head.

"He made a steady wage, but he'd occasionally come home with extra money, sometimes thousands. He told me a successful investment had paid off, and I was stupid enough to believe him. He helped me get the business off the ground. I thought it was wonderful. How many partners come home having made an extra two thousand dollars that day?

"Things went well for several years. And then gradually they started to change. Tom became sullen and aggressive. He was secretive and evasive. I thought he was having an affair, and I accused him of seeing someone else. He denied it, but I was convinced I was right.

"He was always the one who looked after our money and paid the bills. But one day I got a telephone call from the bank saying our mortgage payment had been rejected due to insufficient funds. For the first time in months, I checked our bank accounts. All our savings had gone. All our accounts were empty. I couldn't believe it. I assumed he'd taken it out and was planning to leave me, so I confronted him. That's when he broke down and told me everything.

"He'd started online gambling, and for a while he'd done well. But then it had all started to go wrong. He'd been laid off from his job at the bank a whole year before. A year! He'd gradually gambled more to try to make up the loss, lost more and more, and wiped out our accounts. We had nothing left."

"Jesus," I mutter. It's hard for me to imagine how a person could reach that stage. I've been lucky enough to have always had money in adulthood. How must it have felt that day to see all your balances at zero?

"He broke down and cried. Swore he'd change if I'd help him. Oddly, at the time the main emotion I felt was relief he wasn't having an affair. I promised we'd work through it together. We went to see the bank, who extended our loan and lowered our payments. But after a few months it became clear to me it wasn't going to work. I couldn't make enough money to pay all the bills. I took a couple of other jobs, but Tom was having trouble finding work, and he'd sunk into a deep depression. Eventually we decided—I decided—to sell the house and repay the home loan. Luckily the house hadn't devalued in the time we owned it. We paid off the mortgage and had a few thousand left over. We decided to move away and have a fresh start."

I can see from her thin, pale face that it's not gone as well as she'd hoped. And now she's pregnant, so there are going to be three mouths to feed. My heart aches for her.

I know debt is a black hole from which it's so hard to escape. I wish I could give her a couple of hundred thousand and make all her troubles go away, but I know that would never work. For a start, she'd never accept it; nobody's as proud as someone who's poor. And I wouldn't want her partner getting his hands on it, either.

The man deserves pity, I'm sure. Addiction of any kind is a curse, and it's not his fault, any more than it's an alcoholic's fault that he can't stop drinking. Still, I can't summon any sympathy for the guy. A man should put the woman in his life before anything else. He should treat her as a princess, and make sure she never wants for anything. That's what I would do with Abby, if she were mine.

But she's not, and all I can do is sit and listen, and hope that somewhere along the line I can think of a way I can do more.

Chapter Six

Abigail

Noah sips his coffee and looks out of the window. I can't tell what he's thinking. No doubt it's that I'm an idiot to have stayed with Tom.

But he says, somewhat gently, "I can't think of a better place to attempt a fresh start than the Bay of Islands. It has healing qualities, I think."

I'm so relieved he isn't criticizing me that tears sting my eyes. I was all ready to be defensive if he mocked me or said I was crazy. His kindness is going to be my undoing.

"You must love him very much," he says.

A tear trickles down my cheek, and I wipe it away. He doesn't look embarrassed. He'd make a good counselor, I think. I bet he's the heart of the operation at the Ark. All the others must come to him with their problems.

"I hope Tom realizes how lucky he is," he states.

I finish off my tea. I don't want to talk about how Tom and I feel about each other. I'll collapse into a sobbing heap if I do that.

"I was thinking," I announce, changing the subject. "Izzy offered me a tour of the Ark."

"That was nice of her. I'm sure she'd be delighted."

"Mm. Except I wondered whether you'd like to do it instead."

His eyebrows rise. He studies me for a moment.

"You mean me give you a tour?" he says eventually.

"Yes."

He puts down his empty mug. "I'm a bit busy today."

"No you're not," I scold. "You told me you didn't have much on this afternoon."

His expression turns wry. "I was being polite."

"It's your Ark, Noah. Your sanctuary. I'd love it if you were the one to show me around."

He hesitates and looks out of the window. I study him for a moment; his short graying hair, his clean-shaven face with his strong jaw and straight nose, his violet-blue eyes. He's been so nice to me. I want to give him something in return, but I doubt that I'm going to be the one to change his life.

His gaze comes back to me, and to my surprise there's a firm determination there. "All right," he says. "Let's do it."

My heart races as we get to our feet. I can't believe he's agreed to go outside with me. We bring our mugs and plates through to the kitchen and place them in the sink, and then we don our coats and shoes.

"Are you going to take the dogs?" I ask him.

"No, I'll leave them in the conservatory." He takes them back in there, opens the door into the garden so they can go out if they need to, then shuts the door into the house.

He comes back over to me, and we walk to the front door. We stop when we get there, and he puts his hand on the handle and opens it.

I step outside, then turn to look at him. He pauses on the doorstep, looking down at the ground.

I lift my face to the sun. It's gone midday, and it's warmer now than it was this morning. We could probably go out without a jacket. The sun shines down solidly, and the breeze brushes across my face like a feather, bringing with it the smell of the sea.

I open my eyes and move a bit closer to Noah. Then I reach out a hand and take his in mine. "Just a few steps first," I say. "It's beautiful out here. Come and feel the breeze."

He lifts his gaze to me, and my heart misses a beat. This man is so vulnerable on the inside, and yet there's something about him that's strong and solid and dependable. He's like a wounded animal, a lion or a bear that's lying on its side, and you want to help him but you're nervous about going too close.

He looks down at our hands. "Nobody's held my hand for ten years," he says.

"Oh, I'm sorry." I hadn't even thought about it. I suppose it's too intimate a gesture, especially to someone who's been alone for so long. I wait for him to withdraw his, but he doesn't. Instead, he steps outside.

He takes a few steps forward with me, stopping in the middle of the drive.

He looks relaxed, and yet I can feel how defensive his posture is, with his elbows pressed to his body, his fingers tight around mine, his spine rigid. His chest rises and falls quickly with his rapid breaths.

"You can smell the sea," I say. "I bet it's beautiful in the morning when you walk on the beach with the dogs."

He swallows and nods. "It blows away the cobwebs."

"My grandmother used to say that."

"Mine too." He closes his eyes, breathes in deeply, and blows out a long breath.

I know right now that he's not going to be able to walk all around the Ark with me. It's a step too far. It doesn't matter that he was able to go out during the cyclone. He was needed then, and his sense of duty outweighed his fear. But his agoraphobia has reasserted itself, as if he has a wire wrapped around him that tightens with each step he takes.

But maybe we can work up to it. "That's a beautiful oak tree," I say, pointing to the huge tree in the field that overhangs the pathway to the Ark about halfway along. "I'd love to collect a few oak leaves. Will you come with me?"

He looks at the tree, then at me, and then nods. Slowly, as if each step takes him a great amount of effort, we begin to walk.

"So what gave you the idea for the Ark?" I ask him. "Have you always loved animals?"

"No more than anyone else, I suppose. I never wanted to be a vet like Hal and Stefan. We had dogs at home when I was a teen and Mom first married Matt, but that's about it."

"When was the Ark built?"

"About five years ago now."

"And your wife died ten years ago?" I'm not sure if he minds talking about her, but he nods.

"Yes. The agoraphobia kicked in shortly afterward. I don't know why. I never had it when I was young. It was the grief, I suppose. It just got worse and worse. I was bad for a few years. But time heals, and eventually I started coming out of it."

It's so quiet here. There are three sheep in the field. I wonder whether they've been rescued. Over at the Ark, someone's driving their car into the car park. A dog barks way off in the distance, and I can hear a couple of people laughing, which brings a smile to my face. Other than that it's still and beautiful. The animals must feel so restful and relieved when they're brought here.

"I started painting again," Noah says. "Dad got me a commission to paint a mural at the local SPCA office. I was in the middle of painting Noah's Ark, and I got talking to the guy who ran the office. He was really interesting, and he opened my eyes to the plight of rescued animals and said how difficult it was to rehome them. He hated the fact that they had to put them down sometimes because they couldn't find them a home, and they didn't have the facilities to keep them. And that got me thinking."

We reach the gate beneath the oak tree and, without discussing it, I release his hand and we lean on the gate, looking across at the field.

"Matt has made a lot of money from his books," Noah says. "And with his brothers, they made a fortune through the Three Wise Men business. They funnel a huge portion back into medical research, and also into charity through their We Three Kings foundation. They're very generous with their money. And even though I wasn't Matt's son by blood, he paid for me to go to art college, and then created a trust fund that became mine when I was twenty-one. It was so much money, Abby. And I knew I had to do something with it."

I can't even imagine having so much money you don't know what to do with it.

"Lisa and I talked about it a lot," he continues. "She was the one with a thing about animals. She worked for the World Wildlife Fund, and was involved with saving Maui dolphins, and stopping plastic pollution. She was fiercely passionate about it and swept me up with her enthusiasm. We had all these dreams of ways we could get involved."

He clears his throat. "Anyway, about six years ago after talking to that guy at the SPCA, I just kept thinking about the idea of running an animal sanctuary. I couldn't get it out of my head. It seemed like the perfect way to honor Lisa. Hal, Stefan, and Izzy were on the verge of becoming qualified vets. Leon, my brother, was finishing business school. Albie, my other cousin, was a tech whiz. I began to think how we could all work together to make it happen."

"Where on earth did you start? I can't imagine how you'd even begin to get something like that rolling."

"It was easy once we decided to go for it. I spoke to Hal, Leon, and Albie first. I think they felt the same as me about money. Grateful but guilty. We all wanted to give something back. I looked for a site and came across this piece of land overlooking the bay, and it just seemed perfect. It started as a small vet center, just a couple of rooms, and a building for the rescued animals, and grew from there. We added Ward Seven—the recovery room, and the rehoming center. Then Hal's sister Jules had the idea for a grooming center, so we built a room for that. We had the office block built because it's surprising how much paperwork is involved in the running of a foundation. Initially we began by funding it out of our pockets, but Leon knew that wasn't sustainable. He wants it to be self-sustaining. We're nearly there. We get lots of donations from local businesses. It's really come along since it started."

"It's an amazing enterprise," I tell him. "You've done wonders, Noah."

He scuffs the floor with his toe. "The others do all the hard work."

"Aw, come on. You painted the place, didn't you?"

He smiles. "Yeah, I did all the murals. I'll take you to see them one day."

I'm pleased he's acknowledging it will happen in the future. "I bet they're fantastic."

"They're among the best I've done. I'm pleased with them."

Some of the tension has gone from his body. He's relaxed, standing here talking. I know better than to push him to go further. He's done well today, to get this far.

"So you obviously felt well enough to get out and about?" I ask him gently, still not sure how much he likes to talk about it. "What happened?"

He shrugs. "After the initial buzz wore off, the agoraphobia just crept back. Like the tide coming in."

"Has the depression returned?" I've had a lot of experience with depression. Tom has been severely depressed in the past. It's not easy to live with.

"No," he says. "I don't see it as clinical depression."

"You've never self-harmed or tried to take your own life?"

It's an intimate question, I know. But the moment feels so special. Noah has opened the armor he wears just a fraction and let me slip inside, and I don't want to waste this moment.

He looks at me, and I can see from his sharp eyes that he suspects I have experience in this area. He looks away again, at the sheep grazing in the field. "Sometimes I've thought it would be easier not to be here. To get rid of the pain and loneliness. But I've never considered it seriously. Life is a gift. That's why they call it the present." He smiles.

"Joan Rivers said that, I think," I tell him.

"I heard it was Oogway from *Kung Fu Panda*."

We both laugh.

"I think I'll walk back, if that's okay," he says.

"Of course." We turn and begin walking along the pathway to his house.

To get rid of the pain and loneliness. He's lonely. And I think he's locked into a behavioral pattern, and he doesn't know how to get out of it. So he's just kinda given in. He loved his wife, and he misses her. Maybe he feels guilty he's still alive, and resentful toward the world that she's not. I can understand all those feelings.

"Does Tom self-harm?" he asks.

I look out to sea, at the boats sailing away from Paihia, out toward the horizon. They'll be bringing back snapper, or a kingfish, if they're lucky. "Not at the moment. He did. He was severely depressed. It's one reason I agreed to move. I thought a fresh start would be what he needed."

"But it hasn't worked?"

"A little, I suppose. He's done some financial consulting, but hasn't found anything permanent yet. He really needs to fill in with some manual labor or something, anything to bring in some money, especially now I'm pregnant. But he thinks he's above that." I stop. I'm sure my resentment is obvious enough without me slagging off my partner to an almost-stranger.

"You must think I'm so stupid," I blurt out, resting my hand on my bump. "Getting pregnant at a time like this."

"Not at all. I can't think of a better way to celebrate a fresh start than with a new life."

Tears blur my eyes. "It wasn't like that at all. It was an accident. I'd never have been foolish enough to knowingly have a baby when things are so up in the air."

I stop walking, overcome with emotion. "I'm not saying I don't want the baby," I tell him desperately, conscious that he's lost a child. "Not at all."

"I know."

"I didn't mean for it to happen." I don't want him to think badly of me. I don't want him to think I'm stupid for having unprotected sex when I'd just lost my house. But I can't tell him the awful truth. I've spilled too much already, and I don't know him that well.

"I don't judge," Noah says. "I wouldn't do that. I can't presume to know your situation. You seem sensible to me, and I'm sure you're going to be a wonderful mother."

My eyes fill with tears. "Thank you for the walk. I'm glad you came with me. I'd better go now, though."

His expression softens. "You sure you don't want to come back in for another cup of tea?"

"No, thank you. I'll see you Monday." I walk away, get in my car, and drive off down the lane, watching him in my mirror. He has opened his front door and is standing on the threshold, looking after me. Then he goes in and closes the door.

I swallow hard and dash away my tears. *I'm sure you're going to be a wonderful mother.*

"I hope so, Peanut," I whisper. "I hope so."

Chapter Seven

Noah

After Abby's next two visits, we have a coffee together, then take a walk. Each time, we go a little bit further, although we don't quite make it to the Ark. I have to build up to it. She seems to sense this, and doesn't push me.

I look forward to that hour or so after she finishes her work. In fact I look forward to the whole morning. I love hearing her singing as she moves around the house, or as she's ironing my shirts, listening to music with her earbuds in. And I love her cooking, and her delight in the kitchen and all the ingredients. After she discovers I like spicy food, she cooks me a Thai green curry and then an Indian Dopiaza. Each time, I give her two portions to take home, along with a few of the muffins from the batch she's made that day. She doesn't argue, just places them quietly in a bag.

But most of all, I look forward to the cup of coffee and a muffin after she's finished cleaning. I organize my meetings and phone calls so I'm free at twelve, so we can sit and talk, and then take a short walk in the sunshine.

She doesn't hold my hand again. I know she only did it the first time because she was physically trying to encourage me out of the house. But we walk closely together, and each time I treasure those moments of peace and contentment.

We talk about lots of things. She asks me about the World Wildlife Fund, and the work that Lisa and I did for them. I ask her about The Mad Batter and what kind of cakes she's made, and she tells me about all the kids' birthday cakes she's decorated, in the shape of Buzz Lightyear, Pooh Bear, and Princess Elsa.

We don't talk about what happened to Lisa. And we don't talk about Tom.

I do ask her about Peanut, gently probing to see how she feels about being thirty-seven weeks pregnant, and what preparations she's made for the birth. Her replies are stilted and awkward. When I ask if she's painted the nursery, she says yes, although she doesn't describe it, and I think she's lying. It occurs to me that she might not have a separate room for the baby—perhaps she lives in a one-bedroom apartment. I know she's renting. I ask her if she's enjoying looking at the newborn clothes because Lisa loved that so much, checking out the onesies and the cute hats, and the amazing amount of equipment it seems necessary to have nowadays for something so little.

Abby's somewhat curt answers tell me she doesn't have any of that. She admits she's found some nice pieces in the charity shop, then changes the subject.

I know I'm privileged. Extremely privileged. I don't know exactly how much money I have, although between our fathers and us all at the Ark it's billions. I've never had to fear I can't pay my rent. Or that I won't be able to feed or clothe my family. I knew those problems weren't isolated to the countries of the Third World, but it's not until now I truly understand what a terrible struggle life can be for the ordinary person, even in a country like New Zealand.

Of course, it's been this way for the majority of families in the world for generations. Kids don't need expensive toys and clothes and special equipment. As long as they have a good home life, they grow up just fine. There are plenty of studies and thousands of people who would argue their simple lives have made them more content than some rich spoiled kids who can have anything they want but don't appreciate it.

They say money can't buy happiness. I partly agree with that. It doesn't guarantee it. Even with all the money I have, I wasn't able to save Lisa. It doesn't buy good health or luck.

But it does buy an awful lot. It can buy pleasure and fun. It can buy medical treatment and a nice quiet home and good schools for your children. And it can buy security and comfort. In the past, I've taken those things for granted. For the first time, though, I appreciate everything my money has given me.

When Lisa was pregnant, she spent hours flicking through catalogues showing me beautiful tiny outfits, fancy pushchairs, and all the items many moms use to make their lives easier. We spent a long time designing the nursery of our house in Auckland, making it exactly as we wanted. We bought every piece of equipment going, whether we thought we might need it or not.

But Abby doesn't have any of that. It's going to be hard for her. She's not going to be able to spoil the baby with gorgeous clothes and toys. And from the sound of it, she's not even got the love of an adoring husband to make up for it.

I want to wave a magic wand and make things better for her. But I can't do that. All I can do is be her friend and give her support if she asks for it.

On Friday, we sit and have our tea and muffins as usual, and then I ask her, "Do you have to rush off today?"

She glances out of the window. I wonder whether she's thinking about Tom at home, moody, sulky, and bad-tempered, judging by the little she's told me about him. "No," she says. "No hurry."

"Then maybe we'll see if we can make it to the Ark," I announce. I finish off my coffee with a hesitant smile.

She gives a delighted grin and hurriedly eats the last piece of her muffin. "Come on then!"

We don our coats and head out of the house, walking slowly along the path to the Ark. The weather's not quite as nice today; there's a touch of rain in the air, and the sky and the sea are both the same shade of gray, but it smells fresh, and I take deep breaths, letting the sea breeze calm me.

"What made you decide today was going to be the day?" she asks.

"I've been thinking about it a lot. Working up to it, if you will." I give her a sidelong glance. "One of my therapists suggested meditation, and I've been giving it a go."

I thought she might laugh, but she doesn't. "That's a great idea," she says with enthusiasm. "I'm sure focusing the mind is really helpful in situations like yours."

"I think it's helped. Well, here I am, anyway, so something worked."

"Focus on me," she tells me. "I need something to take my mind off the birth. Introducing me to everyone will really help me."

"Okay." I nod with determination as we get to the end of the field—the furthest we've walked so far. "Let's do it."

We skirt the end of the building and reach the large square in front of the Ark. The veterinary center closes during the lunch break to enable the vets to have time to see to any rescue animals, but the place is still relatively busy, with cars coming and going from the car park, someone taking their recently groomed dog back to the car, Fitz and Leon standing talking by the office block, and Izzy crossing the square in the direction of the other half of the demolished building.

She stops and alters direction as she sees us, her face lighting up. "Noah!" She comes over to me and kisses my cheek. "How lovely to see you." She turns her bright smile on Abby. "Hello Abby. Is Noah giving you a tour?"

"Yes, we've been building up to it for a few days." Abby bites her lip as if she's worried she shouldn't have referred to my affliction, but Izzy just smiles.

"How lovely. Hal's out on call, but Summer is in the vet center."

"Summer's here?" I query.

"She's been in this week, just for an hour or so a day," Izzy says. "You know we can't keep her away."

"All right, thanks. We'll start there, then, in a minute." We say goodbye to Izzy, who heads for the break room. "Summer's my cousin by marriage," I tell Abby. "She's not been well. She has cystic fibrosis, and five weeks ago she was hospitalized with a chest infection, and we nearly lost her."

"Oh, jeez."

"Yeah, it was pretty scary. She's supposed to have a couple of months off, but I knew we wouldn't be able to keep her out of the clinic. Come on, let's say hello to my brother first." I head across the square to the two men in suits standing by a block of buildings to our right.

The guys glance at us as we approach, and the eyebrows of the man in the middle rise. "Noah!"

"Hey." I shake Leon's hand.

He claps me on the arm. "Good to see you out and about."

"I'm giving my friend Abby a tour. Abby, this is my brother, Leon, and this is Fitz, our estate manager."

They both shake hands with her. I watch a pink bloom spread across her cheeks. That interests me. Why's she blushing?

"Good to meet you," Fitz says. "Hey, Noah, can I catch up with you later about some of the building work?"

"Absolutely. Two o'clock?"

"Sounds great—I'll come up then."

We say our farewells, then I gesture to the veterinary center, and we head over there, steering clear of the building site on our right as we cross the square.

"Are we really friends?" Abby asks me.

I look at her in surprise. Is that why she blushed? "Of course. Or is that too presumptuous?"

"No, not at all. I'm just… touched."

"I consider you a very good friend, even though we haven't known each other long. You'd be surprised how much you've helped me."

She looks at the ground as we pause outside the door, then lifts her gaze to me. "Are you feeling okay?"

"I'm concentrating on you like you suggested," I tell her. "That helps." It's true. Thinking about Abby is helping me keep a lid on the anxiousness that bubbles away under the surface when I'm out of the house.

She lifts her gaze to me, and I catch my breath at the look in her brown eyes. For a long moment, our gazes lock, and I can't tear mine away.

This isn't a relationship that can go anywhere, I know that. For a start, I'm not good relationship material. My wife and baby died, and it sent me halfway to being crazy. I don't leave the house. I couldn't take a girl out for a meal or to the cinema or away for a weekend to an expensive hotel.

And anyway, it's likely it's only because Abby's feeling vulnerable and a bit low from the problems she's had that she's reacting to the first bit of kindness someone's shown her. I mustn't mistake that for a genuine affection. And even if it is, she has a partner, and she's pregnant. I mustn't get in the middle of that. For the baby's sake, she needs to try to make it work with Tom.

And yet her eyes are filled with longing and sadness. Unable to stop myself, I lift a hand and tuck a stray strand of her hair behind her ear. Just that innocent touch is enough to make a tingle run down my spine. Her lips are full and pink. They'd be soft if I pressed mine to them. I haven't kissed a girl in ten years.

I loved Lisa—still do—with all my heart, and I'd give anything to have her back. But she's not coming back. And I've missed having a woman of my own. I've missed kissing. Missed making love. Suddenly, I long for it so much it makes me ache.

"Why aren't you married?" I ask Abby before I think better of it.

She gives a little shiver from my touch. "Tom doesn't believe in it."

The fucking idiot. I want to walk into her house, thrust the guy up against a wall, and force him to see sense.

Her eyes glisten. "You make me feel special. Like I'm a snowflake you've caught on your hand."

"You are special, Abby. Incredibly so. And if he doesn't realize that, he's a fool."

She swallows hard and rips her gaze away.

"Sorry," I whisper. This is inappropriate, and I'm not helping her situation. I have to keep my feelings to myself, or I'm only going to make it harder for her.

Anxiety rises within me, tying my stomach in a knot. I clamp down on it, determined to keep it under control while I'm with her. I'm showing her around; that's the only reason for this outing. And the sooner I finish, the sooner I'll be able to go back home to my quiet living room and my dogs.

Chapter Eight

Abigail

Noah pulls open the door and walks into the veterinary center. I don't move for a second, still reeling from his words. My heart's racing, and Peanut gives a celebratory leap inside me.

Noah likes me. My skin still tingles from where he tucked my hair behind my ear. *You are special, Abby.* He thinks I'm special.

And then, as if my positive balloon has been popped with a pin, I deflate. So what? I might not have known him long, but already I can tell there's no way he'd do anything inappropriate while I was pregnant with another man's child. While I was living with another man. And neither would I. I'm just starved for affection, and we're both lonely and hurting. That's all this is, and I mustn't be foolish enough to read more into it.

And yet… I can't deny the way my heart speeds up when he looks at me. How much I enjoy his company, and how much I adore his gentle, kind nature. But then, again, that's probably because I'm having trouble with Tom, and I'm just reacting to the first nice guy who's come along.

Conscious I can't wait outside any longer or it's going to look odd, I push open the door and go inside.

I'm in a large foyer with seating along one wall for clients, although it's empty at the moment. The walls are covered with a beautiful mural, with domestic animals like cats, dogs, and guinea pigs, to wild animals like tigers and giraffes, all mixed together. It's bright, colorful, and exquisitely painted.

Noah's talking to a woman in a blue uniform at reception. He glances over, and I pin a smile on my face. "What an amazing mural," I tell him. "You are so talented."

He gives a modest shrug. "There's a lot of feeling behind it. It had only just been built, and I was proud and excited to get going. Abby, this is Em, one of our amazing veterinary nurses."

We say hello, and he gestures with his head for me to follow him. I walk past the stands bearing dog leashes, feeding bowls, and anti-flea tablets, past the heaps of cozy cat and dog beds for sale, and into one of the treatment rooms.

It has a big stainless-steel table in the center, but there are no animals at present. A tiny, dark-haired woman a few years older than me sits on a stool at a high table, tapping into a computer. As we walk in, she glances up, and a huge smile spreads across her face. I like how everyone's so pleased to see him. She rises and gives him a big hug. I watch him return it, touched they're not worried about showing affection in front of people.

"What are you doing at work?" Noah scolds as they move back. "You're supposed to be resting."

She waves a hand dismissively. "I get bored staying at home. I'm not doing much, anyway. I'm not doing regular clinic hours. Just reorienting myself, you know?"

"Yeah, I know. Zach know you're here?"

Her expression turns exasperated. "Yes, and Dad and Brock. Nobody's going to let me get away with anything." She rolls her eyes at me as if to say, Men! Then smiles.

Noah grins and turns to me. "This is my friend, Abby. I'm just giving her a tour of the Ark."

"Lovely to meet you," Summer says, shaking my hand. She glances at my bump. "Doesn't look as if you have long to go! When are you due?"

"August the third."

"Ooh, not long then. We'll have to meet up and talk babies."

I laugh, genuinely pleased. "That would be great. I haven't been in the bay long enough to make any friends with children."

"Well, mine are growing up now, nine and eleven, but I'm still happy to chat."

"You'll have to come over for lunch one day," Noah says. "Abby helps out around the house, but she's finished by twelve."

"I'll definitely do that," Summer says. "Maybe I'll bring Izzy and Nix too. Something tells me it won't be long before there's more than one pair of tiny feet pattering in the Ark."

We smile and say goodbye, and Noah leads us out of the vet center and back across the square.

"She's nice," I say.

"Summer's a sweetheart."

"Who's Nix?"

"Leon's partner, Nicola. She works here, too. And—oh!" Noah stops in surprise as we exit the building. In front of us, a couple of people are walking across the square. The guy is young and cute, and has his arm slung around the shoulders of the pretty brown-haired woman next to him.

"Albie!" Noah walks quickly up to them and the two men exchange a big bear hug. "I didn't think you were getting back for a few days," Noah says, pulling back, clearly thrilled to see him.

"We were both eager to get back to the Ark," Albie says. "We missed it."

His words please Noah; I can see it. He turns to me with bright eyes and says, "This is one of my cousins, Summer's brother, and his partner, Remy. They've just come back from a holiday in France. Albie, this is Abby, a friend of mine."

We all say hello and shake hands. I feel a touch emotional at being part of this huge family, even if I am on the fringes.

"Did you have a nice time away?" Noah asks.

"It was good to visit," Remy says in a strong French accent. "But I am very pleased to be back in New Zealand." She pronounces it New Zillan', the way Kiwis do, which makes us all laugh.

"Can we come and see you later?" Albie asks. "I'd love to catch up about the new center."

"Of course. I'm seeing Fitz at two. After that?"

"Three p.m.?"

"Brilliant. I'll see you then."

We say goodbye and head across the square.

"You're fond of him," I observe.

"Very," Noah says. "He's a good lad with a heart of gold, and Remy is perfect for him."

"You're like Cupid, aren't you?" I ask suspiciously. "You enjoy pairing everyone up."

He chuckles. "Maybe. It's good to see everyone happy."

"What about you?" We stop and pause outside the office block. Clouds scud across the sky, and a drop of rain lands on my cheek. "Don't you deserve to be happy, too?"

He looks away, across the valley with its rolling green fields and forested peaks. "I had my chance at happiness. I'm content to help others where I can, now."

He doesn't look at me again. He opens the door and goes inside, and I follow him in.

Over the next fifteen minutes or so, he introduces me to a heap of other people. I meet Nix and the rest of the office staff, then he takes me to the grooming center where I meet Hal's sister, Jules, then to the rehoming center where I meet Ryan, and then out and across to the petting farm where I meet Albie's sister, Poppy. By the end I'm a whirl of names and relationships, and as we walk back across the fields to Noah's house, I decide it's impossible to disentangle them in my mind.

The most important thing is that he was able to show me around. After our little exchange outside the veterinary center, he's withdrawn a little from me, and I saw his hands shaking when he opened the door, so I know his anxiety is still there beneath the surface like a riptide, waiting to drag him under. I think our chat might have made it worse, unfortunately. But we talk politely as we walk back, and it's not long before we reach his house.

"Thank you for a lovely day," I say as we go inside. I collect up the bag with the food and pick up my car keys.

"You're very welcome. And thank you for encouraging me. I do appreciate it."

We pause by the door. I hug the bag to my chest, over my bump. "Well, I'll see you Monday, I guess."

He nods and smiles. "I hope you have a good weekend."

"And I hope I haven't tired you out too much."

His smile widens. Our gazes meet, and my heart gives that characteristic leap I'm getting used to when he looks at me.

Then his gaze drops to my bump, as if he's reminding himself that I'm pregnant by another man. "Take care of Peanut," he says softly.

I nod. "See you Monday." I head out of the house to my car and hear him close the door behind me.

*

Another week goes by, and my bump gets bigger. Noah and I still have our coffee and a chat when I finish work, but we keep our talk lighthearted and steer away from anything deep. I don't mind; I find him restful, and he makes me laugh. Which is nice, because there isn't a lot of laughter in my life at the moment.

Tom is in a strange mood, distracted, monosyllabic, withdrawn, and he goes out several times in the week, leaving me to my own devices.

The following Saturday I walk along the beach and collect some shells, thinking that I can make my own mobile for Peanut's room, and paint it bright colors. I wander through the charity shops, knowing I can't keep putting off getting stuff for the baby because it could come early and then I'd be completely stuck, so I buy a couple of bits of clothing, a baby carrier that looks brand new, and a set of feeding bottles. I intend to breastfeed, but it makes sense to keep a set, in case I have any trouble, or want to express. I'll sterilize them thoroughly, and they'll be good as new. My last little treat is a pair of knitting needles and some white wool. I love knitting, and I decide to knit Peanut an outfit. It'll give me something to do, and it'll be another piece of clothing for him or her to wear.

My gaze falls on a good-as-new pram. It's beautiful; navy blue with white piping, the frame shiny and rust-free. Someone's taken care of this. I run my fingers over the waterproof lining of the interior, decorated with tiny yellow ducks. Unfortunately, I don't have the money for it. The only money I do have is in a separate bank account, sitting there ready for me to start up The Mad Batter once the baby's born. It's the only money we had left after we sold our house and paid off the bank, and it's not much, but it should get me back on my feet. For the first time, I'm tempted to draw some of it out to buy the pram. But I promised myself I wouldn't. I need to be able to make money, and if I spend that, I won't be able to start the business. I'll have to find a job, and in the current economic climate, nothing's certain. So I push the idea away.

I've spent nearly all my spare cash. I have enough for the next two week's rent squirreled away. So I call in at the supermarket on the way home and spend my last twenty dollars on food. I buy mostly from the store's economy range—packets of rice and pasta, tins of tomatoes and cheap tuna, baked beans, the cheapest loaves of bread. The shepherd's pies I made the other day were so nice that I treat myself to a bag of potatoes and a packet of economy minced beef; I won't have all the herbs that Noah has to make it super interesting, but I'll be able to make half a dozen meals out of it.

I get home, starting to feel tired, and put it all away. Tom's still out; I have no idea where, and I refuse to ring him and ask him. Maybe he's found work. I doubt it, but miracles do happen.

I open the box of muffins Noah gave me. There are two left. Annoyed at Tom, I eat them both with a cup of tea while I watch a movie. Well, I'm supposed to be eating for two. No doubt he's managed to wheedle himself a pie from a mate. The movie's not very good, but we don't have Netflix and can only choose from the free channels, so there's not a lot of choice. I fall into a doze on the sofa, as the light slowly fades.

When I wake up, it's dark, the only light from the reality show on TV. I get up, wondering if Tom woke me by coming in. But the house is cold and empty. Tired and dispirited, I lock up and go to bed, wrapping myself in the duvet to try to keep warm. Longingly, I think of Noah's huge gas fire, and the conservatory that seems to trap the sun, even in winter. The whole house is warm; I think he has solar panels on the roof facing the Pacific.

You are special, Abby. Incredibly so. And if he doesn't realize that, he's a fool.

I fall asleep with a smile on my lips.

*

Tom doesn't come home Sunday. When I get up, I finally give in and call him a few times, but it goes to his voicemail. I don't know whether to be anxious or annoyed.

I don't want this. When he eventually comes back, we're going to have to talk about how he's been incommunicado, because what if I needed him, if the baby started coming? He's got to do better than this. But I don't want the argument, the recriminations. He'll somehow twist it into being my fault, and I don't have the strength to fight him.

When I was younger, we fought a lot, and I gave as good as I got, but he always won in the end. He's smarter than me and could always find a way to turn the argument against me, until I couldn't even remember what we were quarreling about in the first place.

I go out for a walk, refusing to wait in for him, but spend the hour worrying he's come back, so in the end I return. The house is still empty.

I make the shepherd's pie, for something to do, let the mince and potato cool a little, then put it into six plastic containers. I'll freeze them later. I look in the cupboards, wishing I had the ingredients to make a cake. I'd love to spend time icing it, making flowers, piping patterns. I'll be able to make Peanut birthday cakes each year.

I'm actually going to have a baby. It doesn't seem real. I should be glowing with happiness. Tom should be lying beside me, resting a hand on my bump, trying to feel when Peanut kicks. He hasn't done that once in all the time I've been pregnant. He's hardly mentioned the pregnancy at all.

Noah talks about Peanut all the time. He asks if I'm feeling okay. He brings me a stool to put my feet on while we have our tea and muffins. He's asked me about names and what my hopes and dreams are for the baby. My eyes sting a little. Why can't Tom be like that?

I close the cupboard doors and go back into the living room. I don't want to put on the heater because it's expensive, so I go upstairs and retrieve my duvet, and bring it down to wrap around me on the sofa. Then I flick on the TV again, mainly for the company.

I start knitting with the wool I bought yesterday, but it's double knitting, too thick really for the delicate outfit I wanted. Dispirited, I put it aside, curl up on the sofa, and watch the TV without really listening.

*

I can't face getting into a cold bed on my own, so I end up staying there the night. I doze fitfully, waking with an icy cold nose, stiff from being in one position too long. The front door woke me. I check my phone; it's five in the morning.

I push myself up. I hear Tom taking off his boots, cursing as he bangs an elbow. My heart picks up its pace. He comes into the room and walks past me, through to the kitchen. He hasn't seen me.

I don't move, and eventually he comes back in. He stops dead as he sees me sitting there. "Jesus," he snaps. "You frightened the crap out of me. What are you doing? Why aren't you in bed?"

I've got so much to say, I don't know where to start, so I don't say anything. He comes and sits in the armchair opposite me. I can smell him from across the room—B.O., alcohol, and cigarette smoke. He doesn't smoke, so he's been with others who have. And he's been drinking.

We sit in silence for several minutes. I refuse to say anything, and eventually he gives an exaggerated sigh. "Will you just say something?"

"I tried calling you," I tell him.

"I turned off my phone. I needed to concentrate."

"On what?"

He doesn't say anything.

"What if I needed you?" I whisper. "If there was something wrong with the baby?"

He wipes a hand across his face and sighs. "It's not due for another few months, Abby. Don't be so dramatic."

"It's due in two weeks." I'm disgusted that he has no idea. "This is your child, Tom. Yours and mine. You have to start showing some responsibility."

"I didn't want it," he says sullenly. "I told you that. You had the chance to get rid of it and you didn't. It's your responsibility now."

Cold filters down inside me. "That's a fucking awful thing to say."

He tips his head back on the sofa and sighs again. "I'm sorry. I didn't mean it."

"Yes, you did. Jesus, Tom. What the hell's going on?" The ice that had encased me begins to melt as heat rises inside me. "Where have you been? You've been gone all weekend. Is there… is there someone else?" Even as I say the words, I know the answer, because we've been here before. He smells of alcohol and smoke. It's not another woman. "You've been gambling," I whisper. He stares sullenly at the floor, so I know I'm right.

"Where?" I demand.

"A friend had a card game going."

I stare at him. "I don't understand. How could you gamble? We don't have any money."

Still, he doesn't say anything. His gaze flicks up to me, though. He doesn't look rebellious. He looks terrified.

What has he done? How can he have spent money we didn't have? I had no cash anywhere in the house, only the—

I push the duvet off my lap, get to my feet, and go into the kitchen. I open the cupboard door, move aside the box of cereal, and take out the box at the back. It says it holds risotto rice, but it hasn't held food for a while. It's where I hide the rent money. I open it and tip it up. It's empty.

My heart's in my mouth. I go back into the living room and snatch up my phone. With shaking hands, I hit our bank app and scroll down to the account that holds the money to set up The Mad Batter.

The balance is zero.

Tom leans forward, his elbows on his knees, and sinks his hands into his hair.

"You spent all of it?" I whisper.

"To begin with."

I blink a few times. "What do you mean?"

"They let me borrow some to win it back. But the cards were against me. I just kept losing…"

"How much?" He says nothing. "Tom, how much?"

"Five thousand." He puts his face in his hands.

I stare at him. "Dollars?" It might not be much to some people, but for us it's so out of reach, it could have been a hundred thousand.

"I'm sorry." He folds his hands in front of his mouth. "I was so sure I could do it. And I just kept getting deeper and deeper in. One win, and I would have paid it all back." He lifts his gaze up to me. His eyes are wet. "I just wanted to bring you some money, to make it up to you."

Hot, sweet rage floods me. "Really, Tom? Did you think about me for a second while you were away? Did you think about the baby at all?"

He drops his gaze, giving me the answer.

All my life, I've wanted to prove my mother was wrong when she said it would never work out. I've stood by him, refusing to give in, thinking that trying to make my relationship work made me a stronger, better person. Only weak people walk away, I'd thought.

And look where it's gotten me.

I could scream, stamp my feet, throw things, sulk, cry. But it's not going to change anything. He has a chronic disease. I've tried to help him. I've stood by him. Forgiven him multiple times. Tried to get him help. But what do you do when a person doesn't want to help themselves? He doesn't care about me, about the baby. I don't love him anymore. I haven't for a while. The disease has beaten all three of us.

"What are we going to do?" I ask him. "How are we going to pay the rent?"

"I don't know."

I stare at him. "How are you going to pay the money back?"

"I don't know."

"That's not an answer, Tom."

"What do you want from me?"

"I don't know—some effort? Some ideas of how to pay off five thousand dollars?"

"What about that rich guy at the Ark? Could he give you a loan?"

I know Noah would give me the money. But the thought of asking that honorable, loyal, kind man for help, of admitting what's happened to me, makes me want to curl up and die with shame.

Nausea rises inside me. I hold my breath as I fight against it. After a few seconds, it goes away, taking with it all my emotion—all my anger, my determination, my hope.

I get to my feet, walk toward the door, and pick up my keys from the table. Shove my feet into my shoes and yank my jacket off the peg.

"Where are you going?" Tom calls.

I don't answer and open the door.

"You'll be back," he yells. "You always come back."

I go out and close the door.

I walk away, toward the beach. It's still dark, the moon a bauble hanging over the horizon that blurs as my eyes fill with tears.

Chapter Nine

Noah

It's a cool, blustery morning. I walk the dogs at first light, hunching my shoulders against the stiff sea breeze, and I'm relieved when I reach the end of the beach, so I can return to my warm house and shut out the harsh world.

I run through my plans for the day as I climb the track, helping Spike up some of the difficult steps. Willow bounds ahead, egging him on. I'm working on some ideas for the Hands-On unit today, enlarging on the discussion I had with Albie last week. I want to establish contact with the local primary and secondary schools to sow the seed of the idea of working with their learning enrichment centers. I also have a heap of financial reports Leon's prepared for me, and Fitz's bi-annual report on the estate, which will no doubt have suggestions for upkeep and improvements, and I want to read that by the end of the day.

And of course, Abby's coming this morning. My heart lifts, even though I keep telling myself she's just a friend. So what's wrong with having a good friend of the opposite sex? I like her, and I like spending time with her. There's nothing harmful about chatting over a cup of coffee and a muffin for half an hour. She needn't know it's the highlight of my day. Anyway, it's obviously not going to be for long. Soon the baby will be born, and I doubt she'll want to continue working here after that. I expect she'd like to set up her business again. It'll take capital, though, even if she works from home. But maybe she has a little put aside for that.

As I crest the hill and walk across to the house, my mobile rings. I take it out and look at the screen—it says Abby. We exchanged numbers when she started working, in case she needed to change her time or day at all.

I swipe the screen and answer it. "Hey, morning! You're up early." It's only seven-thirty.

"Hello, Noah." She speaks in a whisper. In the background, I can hear the sound of waves breaking on the shore. What's she doing on the beach at this time of the morning? "I'm afraid I won't be able to work for you anymore."

I stop walking. The dogs look up at me, then go off to sniff around the house.

"What's happened?" I ask.

"Nothing. I'm very sorry to let you down. I hope you're able to find someone else soon."

"Abby, forget about the job. How are you? Is the baby okay?"

"The baby's fine. It's okay, Noah. Everything's fine. Thank you for everything you've done. I appreciate you taking me on when you didn't know me."

Now I'm alarmed. Something's clearly happened, and she's not going to tell me. "Where are you?"

"I have to go now."

"Just tell me where you are."

"Bye, Noah." She hangs up.

I stare at the phone for a moment. Then I open the front door, let the dogs in, and go inside.

I stand in the hallway for a long moment. There's only one thing I can do, but it makes my mouth go dry to think about it. But there's no time for my stupid affliction to kick in now. Abby needs help, and I think I'm the only one who can give it.

I put the dogs in the conservatory, check they have water, and open the door to the garden. Then I walk through to my office and open the top drawer of my desk. I stare at the contents for a moment. Then I take out my car keys.

I walk out and through the house to the door that leads into the garage. My shiny new Aston Martin sits inside, and as I press the button to lift the garage door, the car gleams. I bought this for myself about six months ago, and I occasionally start it up and drive it around the Ark, but I've yet to leave the grounds. I haven't been out of the grounds for five years.

Swallowing hard, I get in the car and start it up. It purrs gently. I buckle myself in, then ease the car out of the garage and onto the drive.

I push away the anxiety that's knotting my stomach and focus on Abby. I'm guessing she's on Paihia beach somewhere. That's no small distance to cover, as the beach extends all the way from Waitangi down to the end of Paihia, a distance of several miles, and it's possible she's driven to Opua or somewhere else near the sea. Hopefully I'll spot her car, and at least then I'll know roughly whereabouts she is.

I head out of the Ark and turn onto the State Highway. My palms are sweating, but I press my foot down, drive to the roundabout, and take the turnoff to Paihia.

I drive at a moderate speed, keeping an eye out for her car. The beach is empty, and so are the parking spaces on the road. The sea is gray in the early light, harsh. Fear rises inside me. She hasn't done anything stupid, has she?

I go all the way through town to where the road begins to rise into the hills, but there's no sign of her car. I turn around and start heading back, thinking furiously. Maybe she didn't take the car. She told me she lives ten minutes from the beach; perhaps she walked there. I park up by the pier, get out, and lock the car.

I lean against it for a moment, taking deep breaths. There aren't many people about; a man's walking a dog along the path, someone's opening up the place where you book trips out to see the dolphins. A couple of tourists are out early, taking photos of the picturesque seafront. Someone calls out to a friend from a boat, about to head out fishing, no doubt.

Despite the peace and quiet, my limbs feel frozen, and my heart is racing. I can't do this. The sky seems too high; the world is too big, as if I'm wearing glasses with lenses that make everything appear larger. I'm too small, too insignificant.

I lean on the car, close my eyes, and take deep breaths.

I read an article on meditation the other day. There are lots of ways to meditate, like counting breaths and visualization. This article suggested taking yourself to a place where you feel happy and content.

I take myself back to my conservatory. Warm in the sun, my dogs at my feet. Abby curled up in the chair beside me, her cup of tea resting on her bump, her fingers sticky with melted chocolate from the muffin. She's laughing at something I've said. She makes me feel good. And she needs my help.

I open my eyes again, steely determination replacing the knot of anxiety. I'm going to do this. I can't afford to fail.

I push off the car and head onto the pier. First I look to my left, searching up the beach for any sign of a lone figure. There are a couple, but they're both men. I cross to the other side of the pier and look down the beach. And then I see her. A few hundred yards away, sitting on a bench on the grassy bank under a pohutukawa tree, looking out to sea.

Relief washes over me. I run around the pier, vault over the barricade, land on the grassy bank, and jog down to the seat. I slow as I reach her. She looks pale and unhappy. She's slumped in the seat, her posture defeated. She must be frozen; her hands are reddened, and she's not wearing a scarf or hat.

I stop beside her and drop to my haunches. "Abby?"

She looks down at me, her eyes holding a touch of alarm. She thinks I'm Tom. She blinks a few times, and then focuses on me. "Noah?"

"Hey." I smile.

"Noah?" She says again. "What… why are you here?"

"I wanted to make sure you're all right."

She stares at me. "How did you get here?"

"I drove. I do have a car. It just doesn't have many miles on the clock."

She doesn't smile. She looks as if she can't comprehend that I've gone there for her.

"Honey," I say softly. "What happened?"

Her bottom lip trembles. Her face is clear; she hasn't been crying, but now tears form in her eyes and tumble over her lashes. "I don't know what to do," she whispers, and covers her face with her hands.

"Oh, sweetheart." I rise and sit on the bench beside her, and take her in my arms. She curls into them as much as she can with her bump, and I hold her while she cries.

Oh, it's cold; the seat is freezing my butt, and there's a touch of rain in the air. My ears are numb, and my hands are tingling. But I wait, letting her sob into my jacket, and hold her tightly until the initial wave of tears subsides.

She takes a shivery breath, and I kiss the top of her head. "I'm going to take you back to my car," I tell her, "and drive us to my house, okay?"

She tries to wipe her face. "I need to… to work out what to do…"

"And we will. But first we need to get somewhere warm, and have a hot cup of tea and some breakfast." I get to my feet and pull her gently to hers. "Come on."

I put my arm around her, and we walk slowly back to my car. A couple of teenagers are sitting on their bikes opposite it, admiring it. I give them a wry smile as I open the passenger seat and help Abby in.

I go to the driver's side and get in, start the engine, and turn the heater on full blast. Making sure Abby's buckled in, I reverse out of the car park and head the car back toward the Ark.

"I can't believe you came out to get me," she whispers.

"I care about you," I say. "You're my friend."

"But you left the house and drove all the way here."

"I'm not saying it was easy," I admit. "But I was worried about you. I could tell something had happened."

She snuffles, trying to wipe her face with her sleeve, and I gesture at the glove box. "There's a pack of tissues in there."

She opens it, takes out the pack, extracts one, and blows her nose.

"I want you to tell me what happened, later," I say, "but first we're going to get in, give you a hot bath, and something to eat."

"I'm not hungry."

"I don't believe that, and you have to think of the baby."

Her gaze slides across to me. For the first time, the corner of her mouth curves up a little. "Is this you putting your foot down?"

"Absolutely. My mother used to say that there's no problem that can't be sorted, and I truly believe that. Whatever happened, we'll work it out together."

She presses her fingers to her lips, fresh tears forming. "Don't make me cry."

"I don't care if you cry, Abby. I'm not afraid of emotion. It's important you realize you're not alone. The Ark is a sanctuary for a reason. We help each other there; we're like one big family, and you're a member of that family now. It's not charity. We're friends, and friends help each other out. You helped me deal with my anxiety. Now it's my turn to pay you back. Whatever needs to be done, we'll do. We'll find an answer together."

She continues to cry quietly, and I leave her to it as I navigate the roundabout and take the turning to the Ark. Hal and Izzy's car is already in the car park, and so is Fitz's, but the place is quiet, just a couple of lights coming from the clinic and Fitz's office. I drive along the lane to my house, opening the garage door as we approach, and slide the car inside.

As the door lowers, I blow out a long breath. I made it. I'm so proud of myself. I feel exhausted, as if I've run a marathon. But I found her, and I brought her back.

Now all I have to do is discover what happened and help her to work it out. Solving problems and finding solutions is what I do.

I glance across at her, my heart aching at the sight of her pale, tear-stained face. She's so beautiful. And so vulnerable at the moment. No pregnant woman should be unhappy. She should be laughing, glowing, filled with excitement at the thought of having her baby.

Well, it looks as if she's made the break from Tom. They've obviously had some sort of argument. I hope he hasn't hit her. She's not bearing any bruises, but there are other ways a man can be cruel.

Anger rises within me, but I keep a lid on it. She doesn't need another guy throwing his weight around. What she needs now is TLC.

"Come on," I say to her. "Let's go inside."

Chapter Ten

Abigail

God, I'm in a state. I'm surprised Noah doesn't just dump me somewhere and drive off, glad to see the back of me. I would have. But he comes around and helps me out of the car, holds my hand, and leads me inside.

"Bath first," he says. "We need to warm you up. Then a cup of tea and something to eat."

I don't tell him I couldn't possibly eat at the moment. I feel terribly nauseous, and my stomach is in a knot. Instead, I just nod and let him lead me through the house. He takes me through his bedroom and into his bathroom, which contains a huge, gorgeous, sunken bath. Releasing my hand, he starts running it, testing the water until it's hot, then adding some liquid from a green bottle. The smell of pine fills the room.

"For relaxation," he says. He points to a seat by the bath. "Sit down, before you fall down."

I do as he bids, relieved, almost, to have any decision making taken out of my hands. He strides out of the room and I hear him rustling about in his bedroom. I shiver, as much from emotion as from the cold. I can't believe he left the house and drove all the way into Paihia to find me. It must have taken him a huge amount of courage to do that.

He comes back into the room, carrying some clothes. "I picked the smallest things I own, but they're still probably too big for you," he says. "Try them on and see what you think, or there's a bathrobe on the back of the door."

"Okay."

He drops to his haunches and looks into my eyes. "Abby? Are you feeling okay? Is the baby okay?"

"Peanut's fine," I say with a sniff.

"You're sure? You've felt it moving lately?"

I hold out my hand. He looks at it for a moment, then places his in it. I turn it over so it's palm down and move it on top of my bump. I wait a few seconds, and then there it is—a soft kick.

Noah inhales, going still as a rock. Oh jeez. The poor man. How many times can I torture him in one day? I'd completely forgotten about his wife.

"I'm sorry." I bite my lip. "I forgot."

He lets his hand linger a while longer, then withdraws it and pushes up to his feet. "It's okay. It's good to feel him moving. I'll leave you alone now. Do me a favor though—will you leave the door unlocked? I promise I won't come in, but if you don't feel well, I'd like not to have to break my own door down."

I nod, and he goes out, closing the door behind him.

Blowing out a long breath, I wipe under my eyes, then get up and turn off the taps. I need to get control of myself or he's right, I'll harm the baby. I peel off my cold, damp clothes and place them to one side, test the water, then climb in gingerly. Ooh, it's hot on my icy feet. I'll probably get chilblains now. But after the initial sting, it subsides to a nice warmth, and I lower myself down with a long sigh.

I rest my head on the back of the bath and slide deep into the water. This is heavenly. I can't remember the last time I took a bath. Our cottage only has a shower.

Our. A strange word. It's supposed to imply companionship, togetherness, familiarity, and love. To indicate that a person is no longer alone. How long has it been since I've felt any of those things with Tom?

I can't let myself think about it now or I'm never going to stop crying. It's okay to allow oneself some time to feel emotional, but eventually you've got to get back on your horse and get on with things.

The trouble is, it's like I'm lost in a forest, and I have no idea in which direction to go. I'm completely stuck. I have no money. In fact, Tom owes five thousand dollars to someone. We're not married, so legally speaking I'm not sure if I'm responsible for the debt. But my name is on the rental agreement. On the electricity bill, the rates, the phone. I am responsible for paying those. And my purse is, literally, empty. Well, I think I have about twenty-five cents in there. Possibly a dollar, if I'm lucky.

What am I going to do? If I leave Tom, I'll need to find somewhere else to live, and a way to pay my bills. But I can't get a job, because in two weeks I'm having a baby. Nobody's going to employ a woman who's just about to drop. I was very lucky that Noah gave me the chance here.

Panic rises within me again, and I take deep breaths, in and out, trying to force myself to calm down. *There's no problem that can't be sorted.* Is that true? I think I know Noah well enough to know he's not going to let me go back to Tom without a fight. But I can't let him just give me money. I hardly know the man. I'm his cleaner, for Christ's sake. And I don't want to be someone's charity case. Especially Noah. I don't want him to look at me and feel pity. But what else can he think? I'm such a pathetic case. In his eyes, I stayed with a man who was obviously a complete loser, let myself get pregnant, and now I'm floundering around like a turtle on its back after the tide's gone out. Quite literally, with this bump.

Tears of self-pity sting my eyes, but I refuse to let them drop. Instead, I sit up and wash myself with some of his manly shower gel, then lower my head in the water and wash my hair with the shampoo and conditioner sitting on the bath's edge. I'm anxious about talking to Noah and trying to work it all out, but I can't put it off forever. When I'm clean, I decide it's time to get out.

That's easier said than done. I'm so clumsy with the bump—it's put my center of gravity out. For a brief moment, I contemplate calling for help, but that would be excruciatingly embarrassing for both of us, I'm sure. So I manage to turn onto my knees, then carefully push up and clamber over the edge onto the mat. Thank God, I made it. I wrap one of Noah's thick bath towels around me, almost too exhausted to dry myself, but manage to achieve it.

I towel dry my hair, then take a look at the clothes he brought me. Normally, the cotton boxer-briefs and track pants would have been miles too big, but they fit comfortably over my bump, even though the shape isn't quite right. I pull on the gray sweater he's left me, and that too fits snugly over Peanut, although the sleeves hang over my hands. I roll them up, trying not to look in the mirror, knowing I must look a right sight. His socks are too big, and I've left my shoes by the door, so I'll have to stay barefoot for now.

I manage to find a hairband in my pants, and I twist my hair into a damp bun and secure it, then finally go out of the bathroom.

He's sitting on his bed, his back to the wall, reading on his iPad, although he puts it down as I come out. I realize he wanted to be there in case I called out and needed help. I'm so touched.

"Hey," he says, swinging his legs off the bed and getting up. "Are you feeling warmer now?"

I nod, self-consciously pulling the sweater over my bump. "I must look such a sight, I'm sorry."

His gaze slips down me, a gentle brush, and yet even in my disturbed state, it makes me tingle. "You look amazing," he tells me, with no hint of humor. "Come on," he says softly. "The kettle's just boiled. Tea and toast, and then I think maybe bed. You look very tired."

We go into the kitchen. He's already put my favorite herbal teabag in a mug, and he pours the hot water over it, then extracts two pieces of toast from the toaster and puts them on a plate.

"Peanut butter? Cream cheese? Marmite?"

"Peanut butter, please." I am hungry, although I still feel nauseous too.

He spreads it on, and then carries the mug and plate through to the living room. Flames leap above the fake logs of the gas fire. Above it, a nature program is on the extra-large TV screen, although Noah's turned the sound down to a comforting murmur.

I sit on the sofa. He picks up a big fleece blanket he'd placed on the arm and drapes it around me. I snuggle back into it, accept the mug as he passes it to me, and sip the tea. The bath has warmed me up, but the hot liquid begins to thaw the ice inside me.

He sits in one of the armchairs, leaning forward, his elbows on his knees, his hands clasped loosely. He watches me as I take a bite of the toast.

"How long had you been on the beach?" he asks.

I chew and swallow. "A couple of hours."

He frowns. "You should have called me straight away."

"I only called you in the end to say I wouldn't be in to work," I remind him. I honestly didn't call him to ask for help.

He sighs. I crunch the toast again, swallow, and have a sip of tea. I'm so tired I'm almost asleep.

"Did he hurt you?" Noah asks eventually. His eyes are hard. The thought clearly makes him angry.

I shake my head.

"Has he ever hit you?" he wants to know.

"No..."

One eyebrow lifts. "I sense a but."

I lower the toast onto the plate, too exhausted to keep my arm up. "I don't know what you want me to say, Noah. I don't think I can bear to tell you everything that's happened to me."

"You don't have to. I just want to understand."

"I like you too much, and I don't want you to look at me with pity."

"I wouldn't do that."

"Wouldn't you?" Frustration boils over inside me. "How about if I tell you that Tom's spent the money I'd put away for the next two weeks' rent? Or if I tell you that he was out all weekend, and I had no idea where he was, and he wasn't answering his phone, and it turns out he was at a card game, and he owes one of the men there five thousand dollars?"

Noah's staring at me, and I start shaking again as I continue, "Or how about if I admit that when I agreed I'd stay with him after the trouble we had in Hamilton, he wasn't grateful, or relieved. It made him angry, and he took me to bed and..." I trail off. I can't bear to finish.

Noah blinks. "He raped you?"

I swallow hard. "He'd been impotent for a while. I think the shame and guilt made him feel... I don't know, less manly, I suppose. He assumed I'd feel superior, and maybe he was right. He hadn't been able to achieve an erection for months, and I guess his anger gave him whatever he needed to get over that. It wasn't rape, though. I didn't tell him to stop, and I didn't say no." I don't tell Noah that, at first, I was so relieved Tom wanted me that I was pathetically pleased. The pleasure rapidly turned to resentment and even fear when it became apparent he was taking his pleasure from me with no thought to mine. I don't tell Noah that I think Tom enjoyed my fear.

"He didn't use a condom," I add, "and I got pregnant. It was the last time we had sex. He doesn't want the baby. And he doesn't want me, either. I think it's about time I recognized that the relationship is over, don't you?" I attempt sarcasm, but to my ears, I just sound pathetic.

Silence falls between us. On the TV, a colorful bird is doing an intricate dance to impress a potential mate. That couldn't be less of an analogy of my relationship with Noah. I can't imagine telling him anything that would impress him less than this.

And I do want to impress him. I want him to like and admire me. But how can I expect that when I don't even like myself?

I want him to understand. "My father abused me," I blurt out.

His jaw drops. "Oh no."

"And when I was a teen, a boy at school tried to rape me."

"Jesus, Abby."

"I hate feeling like a victim. All my life, I've tried to regain the power that men want to take from me. I ran away with Tom because I felt I was taking my life into my own hands. I needed to get away from my hometown, from my family. And I've stood by Tom because I've been frightened of admitting to myself that I made a mistake. But I have. Made a mistake, I mean. It's been so hard. I don't want to be a failure anymore."

Noah's face is impassive; I can only imagine what he's thinking. Nausea rises inside me. I put down the plate and mug, get to my feet, and walk out of the living room.

I go back into the bathroom, get down on my knees, and vomit into the toilet. Noah comes in and I see his feet moving around me, and I'm humiliated and embarrassed, but I can't stop. I heave over and over again, until my stomach's empty, and still it won't stop. Water runs, then a cool facecloth passes over my forehead. Oh God, I think I'm turning inside out. My stomach muscles are going to squash poor Peanut into pulp.

When I finally stop, I flush the toilet, then turn and sit on the bathmat. Noah wipes my face with the facecloth, then strokes my hair. Tom would never have come into the bathroom while I was being sick. The thought is my undoing, and I dissolve into tears again.

Noah puts the facecloth in the sink, bends and slides one arm under my knees and another around my shoulders. He's not going to be able to lift me—I'm the size of an elephant, but amazingly he does. I loop my arms around his neck, afraid he'll drop me, but his arms are tight around me.

He walks through to the bedroom, places me on the bed, and tries to extricate himself, but I refuse to let go. In the end, he whispers, "All right, shhh," and he climbs on the bed, moves me across, and leans back on the pillows. I curl up beside him, my arms tucked against my chest, and bury my nose in his sweater.

He strokes my back, kisses the top of my head, and murmurs, "There, there," and "everything's going to be okay." I know it's not true, but his tone is comforting, and gradually I stop crying.

Within less than a minute, the world fades away, and I'm asleep.

Chapter Eleven

Noah

Abby's ribcage rises and falls beneath my hand, her soft breath whispering across me.

I could probably leave her to it now, but I'm loath to rise. I don't want to leave her. I don't want her to wake and find me gone.

Her story has shocked me to my core. You hear stories, of course, about women who are abused by men, but I'm lucky that it's never been a part of my life. The guys I know are decent, loving individuals who would never treat a woman like that.

She thinks I pity her, and I suppose I do feel sorry for her because of what she's gone through, but I also feel an intense admiration for the way she's survived. She has a fierce, independent spirit, and a strong sense of loyalty. She's stood by her partner because she hoped to help him get better, and it's not her fault that he hasn't. The guy obviously has a severe gambling problem, and I know because of what happened to my dad that it doesn't matter how much someone loves you; if you have depression, love isn't always enough to lift you out of the depths of despair, and I'm sure it's the same with alcoholism and gambling. For years, my mother thought she'd failed and let my father down because she hadn't been able to help him, but it wasn't her fault. I blamed him for many years, but my therapists, and Matt to a certain extent, helped me realize it wasn't his fault, either.

I tell myself it's not Tom's fault, and that he deserves pity, but I can't summon any. I feel a deep, burning anger toward him, her father, the boy who assaulted her at school, toward all men who take advantage of women in this way. Because they damage them, physically and mentally. And also because they make women fear us. We're all tarred with the same brush. I hate that schools and colleges are being advised to teach boys 'how not to rape.' As if, left to our own devices, that would be our natural path. That outrages me. And yet, how can I blame women for reacting like that when there are men who treat them this way?

I can't believe that Tom took out his anger and his own shortcomings on Abby. She didn't have to tell me the details; I could tell from her face that even if she hadn't told him no, by the end it wasn't consensual.

Fucking bastard.

Later, I'm going to work out in the gym and punch the living daylights out of the bag.

Against my hip, where Abby's bump rests, Peanut gives a solid kick. Abby doesn't even twitch, but it makes me inhale sharply. The things women have to go through.

I lean my head back, looking up at the ceiling, and think back to Lisa's pregnancy. For most of the pregnancy, she'd been happy and healthy. When she was thirty-seven weeks, I'd spotted that she had some swelling and had tried to get her to rest, but she'd been busy at work, and she'd ignored the warning signs her body had sent her, saying every pregnant woman had puffy ankles. She'd skipped one of her regular weekly checks with the midwife, and by the time I noticed she had swelling in her face and hands, she admitted to me she hadn't felt the baby kick in a few days. We took her to hospital, where they found she had a sudden rise in her blood pressure and protein in her urine. Too late, we'd discovered that her mother had suffered from preeclampsia while having Lisa's younger sister, which meant Lisa had an increased risk of it.

She'd been admitted to hospital, and eventually they induced her. But the placenta had separated from the uterus, causing the baby to be stillborn. Lisa suffered a stroke, and then heart failure. Just a few hours later, despite the doctors doing everything they could, she died.

I'm relieved to feel Peanut's kick, but of course that doesn't mean everything is right with Abby's pregnancy. I'm betting she's not been going for her regular checks. And there's no way Tom would have been bothered to take her to hospital. I can't imagine him going to prenatal classes with her, either. I have a feeling Abby has been so busy trying to keep her life in one piece with both hands that she's not had a chance to even think about the birth or what will happen when the baby's born.

There are a hundred things I could do to help, but I'm not sure if Abby will want me to do any of them. And after what's happened to her, the last thing she needs is for me to waltz into her life and start telling her what to do. All I can do right now is be there for her.

So I lie there, just holding her, trying to lend her my energy and strength, while she sleeps and occasionally twitches, and Peanut twirls around in her womb. I rest a light hand against her bump, feeling the baby moving. I saw my own child after it was born. A perfect girl, ten fingers and toes. At that moment, my heart cracked, and Lisa's death caused those cracks to spread, and then it shattered completely.

Peanut knocks against my hand, and my lips curve up in spite of myself. It's as if he or she is trying to communicate with me. It won't be long, and it will be in Abby's arms. Will Tom want anything to do with it? It sounds as if he's going to turn his back on it. He should pay maintenance, but I can't see that happening when he owes five grand.

I wonder if Abby's responsible for any of the debt. I can only imagine her desperation this morning, when she found out what had happened. How awful to be in that predicament, where you have no choice but to stay.

I lie there, half dozing myself, enjoying the warmth and Abby in my arms. My phone buzzes a couple of times against my other hip, but I ignore it. Willow wanders in at one point and nuzzles my hand, then goes out again. Spike is asleep in the sunshine, no doubt. I hope Abby can draw some strength from the peace here.

She finally rouses around ten o'clock. Opening her eyes, she glances around, confused, then sees where she is, and her memory kicks in.

She pushes up and looks at me. "Oh God," she says. "How long have I been asleep?"

"A while. It's nearly ten."

She looks horrified. "Noah, I'm so sorry."

"It's okay."

"But you're busy, you must have things to do, and I—"

"Abby. It's okay."

She closes her mouth. My arm is still around her, and I rub her back. To my surprise, she leans back against me, resting her cheek on my shoulder.

"We're going to sort everything out," I promise. "But the first priority is you and the baby. I have a doctor who comes to my house if I need him. If I call him and he comes here, would you agree to see him?"

She lifts her gaze to mine. For a moment, I think she's going to refuse, but then she gives a small nod.

"Okay." It's a good first step, and I feel relieved. "I'm going to give him a ring. When you feel up to it, come out and we'll try and get some food in you again, all right?"

She nods again. I rise, somewhat reluctantly, and head for the door.

"Noah," she calls out. I stop and turn. "Thank you," she whispers.

I smile and walk down to my office.

Pulling the door almost to, I quickly check my messages and emails, then dial the number for Brock King. Brock is my uncle, Hal and Jules's father, and for the last ten years, he's been my doctor, visiting me at the house on the rare occasion I've been unwell.

He answers within a few rings. "Brock King."

"Hey, it's Noah."

"Hey, Noah. I was just thinking about you. How are you doing?"

"I'm good. Where are you at the moment?"

"At Matt's. Why, you need something?" My father lives in Russell, just across the bay. Brock lives in Auckland, but he has a beach house up in the bay, and he often visits my father up here.

"A favor," I reply. I tell him about Abby, explaining that she's a friend, she's in trouble, and she's eight months pregnant. "The baby's moving, but she's not been eating well, and she's been distressed. She was very cold when I found her, and I think she's in shock. I'm worried about their health."

I wait for him to ask for more details—how did I meet her, and what's our relationship? But all he says is, "I'll leave now. I can pick up a portable ultrasound from the surgery in Paihia. I'll have to come over on the car ferry, so I'll be about forty minutes, I guess."

My throat tightens with emotion. "Thank you. I ran her a hot bath, and she slept for a while. Is there anything else I can do for her in the meantime?"

"Something to eat and drink, but don't force her. Just reassure her. Keep her warm and calm."

"Okay."

"Noah?"

"Yeah?"

"You're a good lad."

I give a short laugh. At forty-two, it's rare for anyone to call me lad nowadays. "Yeah," I say. "Proper knight in shining armor, me. Thanks."

"No worries. I'll see you soon." He hangs up.

I pocket the phone, go into the kitchen, and open the cupboards. What can I make her? Something warm and comforting… I take out a can of my favorite chicken soup. Worth a try.

I place it in a container and heat it in the microwave. By the time she comes out, it's ready, and I pour it into a mug.

"Hey." I smile at her. She's brushed her damp hair and retied it, and she looks calmer, less anxious than she was when she first arrived. "How are you feeling?"

"Better, thank you. Something smells nice."

I push the mug over to her. "Chicken soup, if you fancy it."

She smiles, picks it up, and sniffs it. "Mm." She takes a sip, nods, walks down the slope into the living room, and sits on the sofa.

I take a couple of bottles of water out of the fridge and follow her. She accepts one from me and has a long drink, then continues to sip her soup. I cover her legs with the fleece blanket. She doesn't say anything, just looks up at me with her big brown eyes.

I walk across to the conservatory, pick up the dogs' water bowl, and take it to the kitchen tap to refill it. I return it to its spot and toss them both a biscuit, which they crunch happily, lying in the sun. Then I come back to the armchair and sit.

She puts down her mug and draws up her knees as much as her bump will allow. "I'm so sorry about earlier. I was a little hysterical, I know." She holds up a hand. "I know you're going to say it doesn't matter. But I'd worked myself up into a state, and I know that's not good for the baby."

I don't say anything, sensing she's trying to gather her thoughts.

"To be honest," she says, looking a little puzzled, "I can barely remember what I said when I got here. I think I blurted out all kinds of things. I feel a little embarrassed about that. It's not really any of your business, and I am sorry to impose on you."

I don't reply, just continue to study her, and in the end her lips curve up. "Stop looking at me like that," she scolds.

"Like what?"

"With mild exasperation. You don't owe me anything, Noah."

"I know. But I'm a decent human being. If I'd met any woman on the side of the road pregnant and in distress, I'd have helped, and you're my friend. Anyway, I do owe you. You got me out of the house and walking around the Ark. That doesn't happen every day of the year, I can assure you."

She picks up her mug again and sips her soup, keeping her gaze on me. I lean back, letting her muse, eventually matching her smile.

"Are you an angel?" she asks eventually.

I laugh. "My mother would say definitely not."

"I've never met anyone like you," she says softly.

I scratch at a mark on my jeans. "I know your experience of men hasn't been great, but all the guys I know are decent men who love their partners, if they have them, and who treat women with respect. I'm nothing special."

"I don't believe that," she says.

She's wrong. But I like that she feels that way, and I don't argue with her again.

Chapter Twelve

Abigail

I sip my soup, keeping my gaze on Noah, who sits back in his chair, also surveying me with a small smile on his lips.

I know that what I told him earlier about Tom and my past shocked him. I'd have said he's quite naïve and has been too isolated up here in his ivory tower, but then I remember that his father committed suicide, as well as both his wife and baby dying, so he's certainly not lived a blessed life.

"Why did your father take his own life?" I ask him. It's a private, sensitive subject, and he has every right to tell me he doesn't want to talk about it, but because of what's happened this morning, I think maybe he feels able to discuss it with me.

"He suffered from severe depression," he says. "He was struggling with it anyway, and then the Christchurch earthquake happened. He and Mom were right in the center of the city when it hit. They lost their house, and I think the trauma of it all tipped him over the edge."

"How... did he..."

"We were staying with my grandparents—her parents. He cut his wrists in the bath."

I touch my fingers to my lips. "Oh, Noah, I'm so sorry."

"Mom found him," he says. "I was eight. I can remember the day quite clearly. It had a profound effect on me. I was quite a rebel in my youth." He smiles.

"I can't imagine that. You seem like the epitome of control and good behavior."

He gives a short laugh. "I was very far from that. I was heading toward a very bad ending. But then Mom moved up to the Bay of Islands and met Matt, and he really turned things around for me. Not just because he had money, although that helped, obviously, but because he was willing to listen, and he seemed to understand me. He'd gone through something similar as a youth—his sister died from an asthma attack when she was young, and he had a few tricky years before he pulled things around."

He has another swig of water from the bottle in his hands. I watch him swallow, see his throat muscles constrict, watch him wipe his mouth with the back of his hand. "Anyway," he says, "we need to talk about you, not me."

"Do we have to?" I sigh as he tips his head to the side. "I'm being flippant. I know I have to sort myself out. I just don't know where to start."

"Let's begin here: do you want to go back to Tom? You're carrying his child. Do you think he might change his ways when the baby's born? Do you want to try and work things out with him?"

"No."

He gives a short laugh. "You want to think about it?"

I turn the mug in my hands. "He's expecting me to run back to him because that's what I've always done. But if I do, I'll be saying it's okay to treat me—to treat women—abysmally. And I don't want to go back to him. I don't love him anymore."

I pause, knowing I can't say that the reason I feel this way is because Noah has shown me what it's like to be with a man who treats a girl right. We're not even dating, and he makes me feel like a princess. How would it feel to belong to this man, to be the one person in his life he turns to? To be loved by him? I can't even imagine such a scenario, because it's so outside my realm of experience.

"But the thing is," I continue quietly, "at this moment, I have no option. I have nowhere else to go."

Noah doesn't look worried. He looks amused. "Of course you do."

"Do you mean a women's shelter? I suppose I could consider that, but I'm not sure how they'd feel about having a woman so close to giving birth, and—"

"No, Abby." He leans forward, his elbows on his knees, and studies me patiently. "You said, 'All my life, I've tried to regain the power that men want to take from me.' The last thing I want to do is waltz into your life and tell you what to do. But I do want to help you work it out. And if you don't want to go back to Tom—if you really don't love him anymore—then we definitely have to find another option."

I bite my lip. I can't see how. With no money and no home, what the hell am I going to do?

"As I see it, there are two options to begin with," he says. "The first is that you stay in a hotel or a motel."

"I can't afford that."

He gives me an exasperated look. "Jesus, Abby. I'd pay for it, obviously."

I stare at him. "What?"

"Honey, I admire you for wanting to stand on your own two feet. But to be perfectly honest, this isn't about you. It's about the baby. You need somewhere safe and secure to have your baby and to look after it. A motel room isn't exactly ideal, but it's better than being on the street, or going back to the fucking idiot you've walked away from." He purses his lips. "Sorry, that kinda slipped out."

I try not to smile. I feel overwhelmed. He's offering to pay for me to stay in a motel? "It's so incredibly kind of you," I tell him, "but I couldn't possibly take money off you."

"Why not?"

"I…" I can't think what to say. He has no idea why that is such a complicated question. "Tom wanted me to ask you for the money to pay off his debt," I say eventually. "I can't tell you how horrified I was when he said that. That was when I walked out. The thought of asking you… I wanted to curl up and die with shame."

His expression softens. "I understand. But pride is a poor excuse for not doing the best you can for your baby."

I'm so confused. My parents had very little money, even though my grandparents—my mother's parents—were relatively wealthy. I knew my mother refused to ask them for money. It was drummed into me. You make your own way—you don't beg from other people.

"It's just money," Noah says. "Bits of paper and circles of aluminum and bronze. You don't think I feel guilty for having more of it than most other people? What have I done to deserve it? It's one reason I opened the Ark. I wanted to help people, as well as animals. We run a free veterinary service for those on low income. We also give huge amounts to charity."

"You don't have to justify your money to me," I say, ashamed. "I know all the marvelous things you do. But it's just so hard to accept charity. Especially…"

He raises an eyebrow. "Especially what?"

Especially from you.

I don't say it. But I think it.

Outside, it begins to rain, dashing against the windows. Inside, though, it's quiet and warm. If I'd still been sitting on that bench, I know I would have started to think that I'd have to go back to the house. There literally would have been no other option. And yet here I am, safe and cared for.

"Would it have made a difference if I were a woman?" Noah asks.

The question surprises me so much, I just stare at him. "Um… I don't know…" But it's not true. "Yes," I admit. "Probably."

"Are you worried about feeling… what's the right word… beholden to me? Because I hope you know me well enough to know I'd never take advantage of you."

"What a shame." The words leave my mouth before my brain has a chance to vet them. His eyebrows rise, and I blush furiously. "Shit," I say. "Fuck. Sorry." I meet his eyes, and we both start laughing. "I shouldn't have said that," I tell him softly. "I mean, I like you, obviously, but…" Dammit. I shouldn't have said that, either.

"The feeling is mutual," he says. "Just so you know. But it's probably best we sidestep that area for now."

My jaw drops. The feeling is mutual? He likes me.

"Don't look so surprised," he says, amused. "You must have realized. I assumed that was why you were worried about taking money from me."

"No… I… what…" My brain isn't functioning.

"I think we're both out of practice with this," he says. "I haven't been with anyone for ten years. I'm a bit rusty when it comes to talking to girls." He smiles.

My head's spinning. Noah likes me in *that* way. I thought he was just being kind.

But he's right, we have to sidestep it for now. That's not our priority right this minute. God, the timing couldn't have been worse.

"There's another option," he says. "You could—" He stops and cocks an ear at the same time that the two dogs jump to their feet and start barking. "That's Brock," he says, getting to his feet. "We'll carry on this conversation later." He walks to the front door.

I can't believe I've felt so many conflicting emotions in one morning. I have to keep my wits about me. I have to concentrate on my plight and the baby. I can't go having romantic notions about Noah King.

For a start, he's the one man who's shown me kindness in a long, long time, maybe ever. I absolutely must not mistake my gratitude for romantic feelings. And yet how do I explain the way my heart leaped when he said, "The feeling is mutual… Just so you know."

Ultimately, though, it doesn't change anything. I have to be careful about accepting his help, because… I look out at the rain-covered garden. Why? Why mustn't I accept his help? He's right; there's no way he'd take advantage of me. He's not going to give me money and then demand I get in his bed. Jesus, of course he isn't. After what happened to his wife, he's just desperate to make sure I'm somewhere safe to have and raise the baby.

Anyway, maybe I could treat the money as a loan. But how would I pay him back? I don't see how I'm ever going to be able to start up The Mad Batter again, and even if I did, I'd barely cover my costs for a while. Hmm. I'm going to have to think about this.

And do I want to have a baby in a motel room? My heart sinks at the thought. But what are the options? I go back to Tom?

"Brought the weather with you, I see," Noah's saying, and I turn to see a tall, broad-shouldered guy coming through the doorway, collar turned up against the rain. He has gray hair and is probably in his sixties. With him is a woman, also with gray hair cut into a fashionable long bob. "Thanks for coming," Noah says as they come in and start removing their coats. "I really appreciate it."

"Of course, not a problem at all." The guy's gaze slides to me, and I get to my feet, smoothing down the sweater over my bump nervously. "You must be Abby," the guy says, coming forward to greet me. "I'm Brock King—Noah's uncle."

"Hal's dad," I confirm. "I met him the other day."

"That's right." We shake hands. He's smiling, but his eyes are sharp, appraising. He's carrying a large black box. "This is my wife, Erin," he says, turning to introduce her.

She comes forward and takes my hand, then places her other one on top of it. "Hello," she says. "It's lovely to meet you. How are you doing?"

"I'm okay," I say, a little awkwardly. I'm thirty-two, but suddenly I feel like a sixteen-year-old.

"Coffee, anyone?" Noah asks, going into the kitchen.

"Please," they both say.

"Another cup of tea, Abby?" he asks me.

"Yes, please."

"Good girl," Brock says. "Keep the fluids up." He glances at Noah. "Okay to take her into your room for an exam?"

"Of course."

Brock smiles. "Come with me."

I follow him through to Noah's bedroom, where he'd held me and comforted me while I slept. It's obvious we've been sitting on the bed as the duvet is rumpled, but Brock doesn't say anything; he gestures for me to get on, so I do, and I turn and lie back on the pillows.

He sits beside me. "Okay, so I don't know what Noah's told you about me. I work part-time as a GP up in the bay, but occasionally I still do some work back in Auckland at the children's hospital. I specialize in respiratory illnesses, and I've worked closely with obstetrics. I'm just going to do a few routine checks and we'll see how you're doing, okay?"

I nod, reassured by his gentle manner.

"Let's get a few details first," he says. He takes out a form and asks me my full name, date of birth, and address. I give the house address, but tell him I don't think I'll be going back there. He just nods and doesn't comment. Instead, he asks about the pregnancy, how far along I think I am, what scans I've had done, how I'm feeling.

Then he opens his black case. He takes my blood pressure, which he says is good considering I'm obviously a bit stressed at the moment. He takes my temperature, listens to my heart and lungs, then listens to the baby's heartbeat. "Strong and regular," he says with a smile, making my throat tighten. "Okay, I have a portable ultrasound here. Let's take a look at baby, shall we?"

I raise my sweater, and he puts on some gel, props up the screen so we can both see it, and places the receiver on my tummy. He moves it around a little until he finds the spot he's looking for. And then there's Peanut. I can see the nose, the round forehead, the ears, the arms up by the head. It's amazing. Tears pour down my face.

Brock just smiles. "Do you know the sex?"

I shake my head.

"Do you want to?"

I hesitate. Then I nod.

"It's a boy," he says.

I press my fingers to my lips. "Oh my God." I'm having a baby boy.

The revelation was just what I needed to make this real. Up until now, Peanut had been a kind of mysterious alien inside me, and it has been difficult for me to picture it as a living, breathing baby. But suddenly I realize that in less than two weeks, I'll be holding him in my arms. A baby boy.

Chapter Thirteen

Noah

I'm sitting talking to Erin when Brock comes back into the living room.

"How is she?" I ask.

"She's fine. She'll be out in a minute." He comes and sits next to his wife on the sofa. Erin's fussing Willow, who has her head on Erin's knee. "Both her and the baby are well," Brock tells me.

I lean back in the armchair, letting the tension go from my shoulders. I hadn't realized until that moment how nervous I was there was something wrong.

Their expressions soften at my obvious relief. "So the baby hasn't suffered because she hasn't been eating well?" I ask.

"Malnourishment can affect an unborn baby's growth, but I don't think it's gone that far. Babies have an amazing knack of stealing what they need from their mom, and it's the mom's health that often suffers. She could do with a good steak, there's no doubt about that. I've given her some vitamin tablets. But there's no sign of preeclampsia, and the baby's heartbeat is strong. It's the right way up, and there aren't any obvious complications."

I stand and walk over to the window, looking out across the garden to the sea. The rain has eased a little, but the Pacific is still a stormy gray.

She's going to be all right. The baby's going to be all right. My emotions feel as if they're out on the waves, being tossed around in the wind. I blow out a long breath, waiting for them to settle.

"Is the father in the picture?" Brock asks.

I turn and slide my hands into my pockets. "He's around, but he doesn't want the baby. She doesn't want to go back to him."

Erin and Brock exchange a glance.

"Those are her words," I say softly. "Not mine. If that was what she wanted, I'd encourage it. Of course I would. But he's been abusive. I don't think he's hit her, but he's come close to it. And he's a gambler. She walked away because he spent her last two weeks' rent money, on the same day that he lost five thousand dollars they don't have."

Both of them look shocked. "Jesus," Brock says.

"This isn't about me and Abby," I tell them.

"It's none of our business," Erin says.

"I don't care, I want you to know. She's my housekeeper. A good friend. We're not romantically involved."

"Not yet," Erin says. I give her a wry smile.

"What are you going to do?" Brock asks.

"I have a few ideas." I turn my smile to Abby then as she comes out. She looks happier and calmer, reassured, no doubt, by Brock giving the green light to the baby.

"I hear everything's fine," Erin says to her. "I'm so pleased for you."

"Yes." Abby lowers herself into one of the armchairs. "It's a big relief. I've not been good in going to my checks, and I have to admit I was worried things weren't quite right." She looks at me then and gives me a shy smile. "It's a boy."

"Oh." Warmth spreads through me, and I feel myself grinning in return. "That's fantastic."

"Well, we'd better get going," Brock says, touching his wife on the knee. "I'm going to be up in the bay for a few weeks, though, so if you want anything, you only have to call."

"Do you deliver babies?" Abby asks.

"I've been present at quite a few births," Brock admits. "But I'm no expert. I know several midwives, though. I'll be happy to recommend one if you'd like that."

Abby looks down, and Brock glances at me. "Thanks," I say softly. "We'll be in touch."

"Okay." The two of them give Abby a kiss and me a hug, and I see them to the door.

When they're gone, I come back in with the dogs, and go down into the living room. Abby's moved back to the sofa, and she's curled up with the blanket over her legs.

"Can I get you anything?" I ask her.

She's holding her tea, and she just smiles. "No, thanks."

I sit back in the chair. "I'm glad everything's okay."

"Me too. I was worried I'd somehow hurt the baby." She looks sad.

"Oh, I think he's very well protected in there. So… you're having a son."

She laughs at that. "Yes! It made it all seem much more real."

"Boys are cool. Much easier than girls."

She grins. "I can believe that."

We sit in the quiet for a while, sipping our drinks. Willow sighs and flops onto her side in front of the fire. Spike sits by me, leaning against my leg, and I stroke his head.

"So…" I say eventually. "Where were we?"

"You had very kindly offered to pay for a motel room for me," she says.

"Mm." I don't like the idea, but I felt I had to offer. "Another option is that I ask around the girls at the Ark and see if any of them has a spare room." I'm sure Izzy or Nix would offer to put Abby up if I told them her story, but both of them have only just entered into new relationships, and I know the last thing they'd want would be a stranger in the house and a crying newborn keeping them up.

"There is a third option," I say. Abby turns her wide, unsuspecting eyes on me. "Stay here with me," I tell her. She blinks a few times. "I have four spare bedrooms," I say. "Several spare bathrooms. You could even use the library as a living room, if you wanted your own space."

"Oh, Noah," she whispers.

"I know it's not perfect. I know it goes against the grain for you to accept help. I do understand that. And I do understand that you're a woman on your own, and it might make you uncomfortable to think you live in my house. But we have to think of the baby. Better that it's born here, in peace and quiet and with friends to help you, than some cramped motel room surrounded by strangers. We could get Brock to recommend a midwife and have her on standby. You could have the baby at hospital, or you could have it here, if you wish."

She raises her eyebrows. "Have a home birth?"

"I don't see why not. Brock said there aren't any obvious complications."

Her mouth has formed an O, and she looks flummoxed. "I don't know what to say…"

"Bear with me. I do have one further idea that might help you make up your mind."

Her lips curve up. "You're full of ideas today."

"It's what I do. I want to help you get back on your feet. I'm sure that's what you want more than anything. So I was thinking… I have an amazing kitchen. I could apply for the license you need to run a business here. Eventually you could start up The Mad Batter again, when you feel able to work, and you could run it from here until you feel in a position to find yourself your own premises. And I had some other ideas. We've been talking at the Ark about sourcing some organic dog treats. That could be something you could look into making—healthy treats for dogs and other animals. Another idea I had is making videos of yourself preparing different cakes. Showing people how to ice them and make pictures. Putting them on YouTube. That would bring in some income if you did it regularly. And you'd be able to sell the cakes."

I'm talking too much—she looks completely shell-shocked. "Or whatever," I finish lamely. "They're just some ideas. I'm sure it's a bit too much for you to think about right now with the baby coming, but when you feel—"

"You'd do that for me?" she interrupts.

"Of course. You're my friend, Abby."

"Are you for real? What… what do you want in return?"

I'm confused. "I don't want anything."

"You're willing to let me stay here, in your house, have my baby here, put up with a screaming newborn, let me work in your kitchen… and all for nothing?"

"Abby, you've been treated abysmally. Your partner has all but abandoned you, left you on your own all weekend when you're close to having your baby. Spent all your money to the point where you can't pay your rent and can't even afford food. He forced himself on you—don't tell me he didn't, because I won't believe you—and then he doesn't want the product of his lust. He disgusts me. I'm ashamed to be a man when I hear about guys like that. Every single one of the men in my family, the men I know, would do whatever they could to help you."

She studies her hands in her lap. "It's not all his fault. I can't call myself a modern woman, a feminist, and then weep and wail when the man in my life doesn't perform the way I want him to."

MY LONELY BILLIONAIRE

"This has nothing to do with gender, Abby. When you agree to be in a relationship with another person, you're telling that person you're going to be there for them, that you'll support them, stand by their side, be their number-one fan. That you'll be strong for them when they need you, and that when you need them, you expect them to step up for you. Relationships are a two-way track. And yours appears to have been entirely one-way. He's sucked you dry, and I'm absolutely stunned you stayed with him so long. I'm stunned at your loyalty, and how much you've given to try to make the relationship work. Plenty of people would have walked at the first sign of trouble. You think that's weak? I think it shows immeasurable strength and compassion. You tried to help him through his problems. The fact that you couldn't doesn't mean you're a failure; it means he's in too much pain and too deep in to be pulled out by anyone less than a professional. He needs proper medical help and therapy. I can help with that, if he'll accept it. But he's not your problem anymore. Now you have to think about yourself and the baby, and that's all. On bringing your child into the world in a safe, secure way. If you feel happy, content, and safe, your son will pick that up from you. That's all that matters right now."

I've said far too much, and I stop as she puts her hand over her mouth and starts crying again. Holy shit. How many times can I make this girl cry today? I'm supposed to be making things better.

I get up and go over to the sofa and sit beside her. Without me saying a thing, she leans against me, and I put an arm around her.

"I don't know what I've done to deserve you," she whispers through her snuffles.

I sigh. "You make me sound like a saint. I'm really not. For a start, I'm so screwed up I can barely set a foot out of the house. I know my desire to help others is born out of a pathetic hope that somehow I can stop everyone else going through what I went through. I want to take away the world's pain, and I'm not stupid, I know that's impossible. But I've got to try."

"You cherish your solitude, though. I know you do. I can't see how having a screaming baby around the house—especially one that isn't yours—is going to help you when you're working or having meetings."

"Okay, well, I'm no expert, but from what I understand most babies don't scream twenty-four-seven. They cry when they want something, and it's our job to figure out what it is. If you're worried about it, you can have the bedroom at the end of the house, right next to the library."

I rub her arm. Despite her big bump, she feels small and slender in my arms. "Also, this isn't completely altruistic. There are several levels to my selfishness."

She gives a small laugh and blows her nose. "I don't believe that."

"Oh, it's true. Level one is that even though I cherish my solitude, as you delightfully put it, I am lonely. When you're here, I like listening to you sing as you work. I like the idea of having you here, and of seeing your baby and watching it grow. All those firsts others talk about—first smile, first time the baby crawls or walks—I missed out on it all. I'm not saying you have to stay here that long, just that I hope whatever happens, we get to remain friends so I can see your son grow up."

She rests her cheek on my shoulder. I look down at her hair and rest my lips on it for a moment. "And level two… I like you, Abby. I wouldn't be honest if I didn't say I'm looking forward to getting to know you better. But I don't know where that would lead. I'm pretty screwed up, and I'm sure that's the last thing you're interested in tackling. I haven't been with anyone in a long time, and I don't know how it would affect me." I still miss Lisa, and I haven't yet thought about how I might feel being with another woman.

I sigh. "And that's just my side. I don't want you to think I would pressure you into anything you didn't want. And I'm also sensible enough to know that now isn't the best time to start a relationship. You're about to have a baby—any woman in your position would be vulnerable and emotional. Those emotions will cloud other feelings, and it's important to wait until the dust settles. And I don't expect anything. I know you don't believe that, but the last thing I'd want is for you to feel that you owe me for this. If, after a week or a month or a year or whatever it turns out to be, you tell me it's time for you to move on, that's fine. I'll be happy. Do you understand what I'm saying? It's important that you do if this is going to work."

She lifts her head to look at me and nods.

"Tell me you understand."

Her lips curve up. "I understand, Noah."

"Okay. Now, I'm famished. I'm going to make myself something to eat—what can I get you?"

She gives me a wry look. "Is this what I can expect? You trying to fatten me up at every opportunity?"

"Absolutely. So let's have something, and then we can talk about where we go from here."

Chapter Fourteen

Abigail

In the end, Noah suggests I stay for a few nights to let the dust settle and to see how I feel about everything. "Stay," he says, "and try to put everything out of your mind and just concentrate on relaxing and feeling better."

Of course, it's impossible to do that. I agree to his offer because I can't think of any alternative. I chew over the decision almost constantly over the next two days.

Wondering if Tom is concerned about me, not wanting him to ring the police, I finally text him to let him know I'm okay. After about two hours, I finally admit to myself he's not even going to bother to reply.

It's the final death knell for the relationship. I know, now, that I can't go back to him—I just can't. It'll be bad for both me and the baby. Whether it was brave or foolhardy, I've made the break. I need to find a way to exist without him.

What other options do I have? I can't afford to fly back to England, and even if I could, I wouldn't want to return to my parents. Briefly, I consider contacting one of the friends I left behind in Hamilton, but most of them have kids, and even though I'm sure they'd help if they could, I can't imagine any of them having the space or inclination to keep me and a newborn.

I think about taking Noah up on his offer to put me up in a hotel or a motel. But I can't think of anything more depressing than returning there after giving birth. I have to think of my mental health. I've always thought of myself as a strong person, confident and resilient, but right now I'm fragile and emotional, packed full of baby hormones, and I have to put Peanut first.

I could go to the local Women's Refuge and exist on their charity. There would be other women who might be able to help me look after the baby. But ultimately, is that going to be any less depressing than staying in a motel?

So… why shouldn't I accept Noah's offer to stay at his house?

I lie awake that night, in the strange bed with the crisp duvet, thinking about Noah sleeping a few rooms down, going over it in my mind. He's possibly the kindest person I've ever met. And I really don't want to take advantage of him.

But then I start thinking that maybe I'm being unfair to him. He's not eighteen, making foolish declarations without thinking them through. He's a grown man—ten years older than me, rattling around in a huge house, stuck in a behavioral pattern he's having trouble breaking out of. He's human, so he's right—his offer isn't going to be all altruistic. Maybe he's seeing this as a chance to do something different. Yes, it's a sacrifice—he's giving up his peace and quiet, and to some extent I know he's going to feel responsible for me and the baby. But I believe him when he says if I wanted to leave, he wouldn't try to stop me.

Why do we always think the worst of people? It's possible there are generous souls out there who only want to help, isn't it? I don't want to be the kind of person who's always looking for the bad in people. I want to trust Noah. And I want to believe there's nothing wrong with me staying at his house until I'm back on my feet. What am I worried about? That he'll take sexual advantage of me? Do I really think the gorgeous Noah King would be interested in me, currently the size of an elephant, decorated with stretch marks, and soon to be covered in baby vomit? Jesus. I should be so lucky.

I pout at the ceiling. I shouldn't think like that. But holy heck, it's been a long, long time since I've had really good sex, the kind that's not painful and where you get an orgasm at the end. Or at the beginning, I'm not fussed. It's been so long since a man's given me one, I wouldn't care at what point in the process it appeared.

I console myself that he hasn't had sex for ten years. Maybe he's forgotten how to do it. Or perhaps he wasn't any good at it in the first place. Then I think about the way he held me, his gentle hands, and I sigh. I'm fooling myself. There's no way the guy isn't a god in the bedroom.

For a brief moment, I consider the fact that this is some kind of twisted attempt from him to recreate the perfect life he had before his wife and baby died. But that's unfair to him. It was ten years ago, for

Christ's sake. He has his issues, obviously, but I don't think he's disturbed enough for this to be anything but him wanting to help me.

But that really is nothing to do with me. That's not what this is about. The question is, what is the real problem with me staying here?

He asked me if it would be any different if he were a woman, and of course it would. If it had been Izzy or Summer who'd offered, I'd still have felt awkward and as if I was intruding, but I would have believed in their generous offer, and I wouldn't be worrying what other people were thinking.

So I suppose the question is, do I believe that every man is rotten to the core?

My experience hasn't been great in the past. But it's different now. I've met Hal and Leon, Albie and Stefan, Fitz and Ryan. They've all been kind, and seem decent, hardworking guys, despite the fact that most of them could probably buy this house ten times over. They all love and respect women. I can only conclude that I've been terribly unlucky. Or maybe I'm just very lucky now. And I would be foolish to let this opportunity, this amazing chance, slip through my fingers on account of pride.

But, lying here in the dark, I can admit the truth to myself. I don't just want to stay because it's a great opportunity. Or because of Peanut. I want to stay because of Noah.

I'll keep it to myself, for now. But I acknowledge and store it close to my heart.

On Wednesday morning, I give him my decision: for the foreseeable future, I'm going to stay.

I don't think he could have hidden his delight if he'd wanted to. His smile is breathtaking, full of genuine pleasure. All he says is, "Cool! Want a cup of tea?" But he continues to smile as he fills the kettle, and I know I've pleased him.

As the rest of the day goes by, I begin to think that this could work. During the day, Noah is busy; he's on the phone, on conference calls, working in his office, or accepting visitors for meetings. People come and go on a regular basis, and it soon becomes clear he's told everyone what's happening, because when I bump into Hal or Leon or Fitz coming out of the conference room or Noah's office, they're warm and friendly, and nobody asks me what I'm doing here.

When there are visitors, I stay in my room, read in the library, or go out for a short walk, down to the beach. Then, when they go, Noah comes and asks me if I want to join him for a meal. We eat breakfast and lunch in the conservatory, while we read. We have dinner in the living room watching the TV.

After that is my favorite time of the day. It's warm and cozy with the log fire on, and the two dogs curled up in their beds. We watch Attenborough's *Dynasties* series, and Noah fetches me blankets and tries to feed me snacks through the evening—popcorn, Maltesers, and tiny bits of cheese and crackers.

It's not a long-term solution. I know that. But for now, I feel safe and content for the first time in a long time.

On Friday, he announces that Summer and the other women at the Ark have asked if they can come around after work. Summer apparently has some old baby stuff in her attic that she wants to bring over to see if I can use, and the other girls are keen to talk pregnancy and babies. He asks me if I'm comfortable meeting with them. I'm a little nervous, sure they're going to grill me about what I'm doing here, but I say yes because they're his friends, they all seem nice, and I'm desperate for some female company.

"I have something to ask you," he says as the hour draws near.

"Oh?" We're having dinner in the living room, eating chili I spent the afternoon making, poured over tortilla chips with sour cream and homemade guacamole.

"Mm." He crunches a chip. "My God, Abby, this chili is amazing."

I grin at him. "It's not bad."

"It's something else. Hot but not too hot. Yeah. Really good. Anyway… While the girls are here, I thought I might go out."

My eyebrows rise. "Out?"

"Mm. I thought I might pick up some stuff for you from the house."

I study him for a long moment. He scoops up some chili with a tortilla chip and eats it, giving me an innocent look.

"You want to talk to Tom," I say eventually.

He licks his fingers. "If he's there, I might have a word. But honestly, I thought you might be sick of wearing my sweaters and that you might like your own maternity clothes."

I don't have a lot of them, but I don't tell him that. I also like wearing his sweaters, but I don't tell him that, either. "I don't know," I say doubtfully, "I don't think it's a good idea. And anyway, are you sure you're ready for that kind of outing? Picking me up was one thing—you were driven by a purpose, and that took your mind off it."

"Knocking Tom's teeth down his throat is a purpose." He holds up his hand as my jaw drops and laughs. "I'm joking. Can you really see me doing anything like that?"

"No…"

"I'll take Leon. He's pretty tough."

"Noah!"

He chuckles. "Relax. Don't you want the bits and pieces you bought for Peanut?"

I put down my dish, my appetite vanishing. "I don't have much, Noah. I'm embarrassed to let you see what little I have."

His expression goes carefully blank. He pokes at the chili with a chip for a moment. Then he scoops up some more and crunches it. "Well anyway, unless you expressly forbid it, that's what I'd like to do."

"I would like a few of my cookbooks," I admit grudgingly. "And some of my shoes." And the last thing I want to do is face Tom again.

"Then it's settled. It'll give you girls some space, anyway. The last thing you'll want is me and the guys hanging around making your life a misery."

His violet-blue eyes study me. He's sitting back in the armchair while he eats, one ankle resting on the opposite knee. His jeans are tight over his thighs. He's wearing an All Blacks rugby shirt, one of the performance fit ones, that clings tightly to his body. Yowza. He has muscles in places I'd forgotten men had muscles.

He wears his masculinity casually, and I wonder whether it's been so long since he's reacted to a woman that he's unaware how sexy he is. It's funny to think that when he was younger, he was a rebellious troublemaker. I'd like to have met young Noah, full of testosterone and sex hormones, running hot.

"Don't look at me like that," he scolds, pointing his fork at me.

"Like what?"

He shakes his head, amusement lighting his eyes. "Everyone will be here soon. I'm going to get ready." He takes our dishes to the kitchen.

I look at Willow, who's cocked her head at me. I poke my tongue out at her. She pants, as if she's doing the same to me.

I suppose I should get ready, too, although I don't have anything I can change into. He leant me another sweater this morning, but as much as I like wearing his clothes, he's right, I need some proper maternity stuff because I do look like a circus tent at the moment.

I'm excited at the thought of what Summer might have found in her attic. Perhaps she'll have an item or two of maternity clothing? She's a lot smaller than me, though. It'll be going from the sublime to the ridiculous. Oh well, beggars can't be choosers. I'm going to have to put my pride aside for a while and just accept whatever anyone is willing to give me. It's all for Peanut.

I turn and look at Noah, who's putting the crockery in the dishwasher, and I catch sight of his tight butt as he bends over.

It's *almost* all for Peanut.

Chapter Fifteen

Noah

Everyone arrives within ten minutes of each other, and soon the house is full of people. It turns out that the girls have decided the evening is going to be a baby shower. Summer's brought heaps of bags with her boys' old baby clothes, and Zach struggles in with a fancy stroller that has a removable car seat. Leon and Hal help him with the pieces of a cot complete with a washable mattress, and Zach and Albie spend five minutes putting it up in Abby's room. Summer's brought heaps of baby blankets, mobiles, toys, and lots of other paraphernalia. The other girls have all brought presents, too. I've told them Abby doesn't have any maternity wear, so they've all bought her some items, as well as new things for the baby.

Abby watches from the sofa as they bring everything in, and then promptly bursts into tears.

"Totally expected," Summer says cheerfully as I hover, concerned. She makes a shooing gesture with her hands. "Go on. You lot get going. We'll sort Abby out."

So I leave her with the girls, who carry the muffins she made earlier into the living room, all talking at once, it seems, while Nix sits next to Abby and gives her a hug, and Remy brings her a drink.

"They'll be fine," Hal advises. "They've got chocolate muffins. I'm tempted to stay."

"There wouldn't be any left for anyone else," Albie tells him, pushing him toward the door. "Come on."

I take my jacket from the hook, give one final glance at Abby, see her laughing at something Izzy's said as she wipes her eyes, and I go out of the door. The dogs adore the girls and are happy to stay with them.

Outside, it's dark and raining lightly. I have Abby's house keys in my pocket. I pause on the doorstep and look out across the fields, into the darkness. Ghosts and memories lie in wait, along with the hope and uncertainty of the future.

"Noah?"

I bring my gaze back and see the guys standing on the driveway. I've told them where I want to go, and that afterward maybe we can go to the local bar for a drink. It will be the first time I've done that since the Ark was built five years ago.

Leon walks toward me. "You all right, bro?" he asks softly. "You don't have to do this."

"I'm okay." I remember Abby's hand sliding into mine that first time we went for a walk, and I take a step out into the rain. "Whose car are we taking?"

"I thought mine," Hal says. "I don't know how much stuff Abby will have, but it's probably got the biggest boot."

"Okay." We follow him to the Mitsubishi he bought recently. I'm shaking, and I'm sure they've spotted it, but nobody says anything. Leon gestures for me to get in the front, and he, Albie, and Zach pile in the back, with lots of elbowing and cursing as they struggle to buckle themselves in.

"Everyone ready?" Hal glances at me as he presses the button to start the engine. I just nod. My hands are clenched into fists, but I'm going to do my best to appear calm.

Hal reverses out of the drive and heads the car toward the main road. I give him the address, and he nods and takes the turn to Paihia.

I take long, slow breaths, and try to concentrate on Abby. She's the reason I'm doing this. She and Peanut. Her baby boy. They need help. I can't let her down now.

"How's Summer doing?" Leon asks as we drive through the dark night.

"Really good," Zach replies. "I couldn't keep her away from the Ark, but she's only doing an hour or two a day at the moment. I think it takes her mind off it, you know?"

We all nod solemnly. Summer's recent chest infection proved nearly fatal, and it was a sharp reminder to us all about the seriousness of her condition.

"She's been looking forward to tonight," he adds. "She loves talking babies. She would have had a third, I think, but in the end we decided two was enough."

"Remy wants four," Albie says. "God help me."

We all chuckle. I'm thrilled he's found himself such a lovely girl. Remy had eyes for nobody else from the moment she saw him.

"Have you fixed a date yet?" Leon asks.

"February. We both thought a hot summer wedding would be nice."

I smile. Hal and Izzy are getting married in September, and Leon and Nix in early December. It will be a year for weddings, and no doubt next year will be the year for babies.

"Thanks for this," I say to the guys. "I appreciate you coming with me."

"Of course," Leon says. "We bring the muscle."

"And the brains," Albie adds.

"I'm not sure what I bring," Zach says, "moral support, I guess."

I grin. "It's much appreciated."

"How do you want to play it?" Hal asks. "You want us all to go in, mob-handed, frighten the crap out of him?"

"Not initially. I'll test the waters first. I'm guessing he's not going to play nice, though. If he's there at all." I hope he is. I want to meet the man who's treated Abigail so appallingly. I'm terrified of being outside, but I'm not scared of the man himself.

Hal slows to check the signs, turns onto a road, and then follows it to the end, where it meets Abby's street. We read the numbers on the letter boxes until we find Abby's, and Hal stops the car.

I look up at the tiny cottage. There's a light in the front window. Tom's home.

"Give me five minutes," I say to them. "Then bring your crowbars and knuckle-dusters."

Hal snorts. "Are you sure about this?" Leon asks.

"No. But I need to do it." I open the door and get out. It's really cold tonight. It never snows up in the sub-tropical Northland, but the rain is hard on my face, almost like sleet.

My heart bangs on my ribs, and for a moment it's hard to breathe. My feet feel frozen to the floor. I'm conscious of the guys in the car, watching me, probably exchanging glances. I can't stay here. Am I going to do this or not?

I turn up my collar, shove my hands in the pocket of my jeans, walk up to the front door, and ring the bell before I can change my mind.

I wait for about thirty seconds. When nobody answers, my pulse pounding, I ring again. Still no answer.

Taking a deep breath, I slot the key in, open the door, and go in.

All the lights are on. I push the door to, walk along the corridor, and turn into the living room.

Tom is on the sofa, asleep. There are half a dozen empty cans of cheap beer on the coffee table. The place stinks of B.O., booze, and cigarettes. He's unshaven, his clothes rumpled.

I glance around the room, looking for anything Abby might want me to pick up. I can't see much of her presence here. A pair of slippers. A couple of older baby magazines put tidily on a shelf in the corner. I should have brought up one of the boxes Hal has in the car.

I pick up the slippers and magazines, the bag of half-finished knitting by the side of the sofa, the small pot of hand cream, the notebook with flowers on the cover and the glittery pen. Anything that looks vaguely feminine. There's an empty bag on the table, and I put everything in it.

"Hey!"

I turn to see Tom blinking furiously, getting to his feet. "What the fuck!" he yells.

I move to put the sofa between us. "I'm Abby's friend. She gave me her key. I'm here to collect her stuff."

He scrubs at his eyes. "Abby? Where is she?"

"She's going to be staying with me until the baby comes. I'm here to pick up some of her bits and pieces to make her comfortable."

"Who the fuck are you?" His gaze scans down me, then back up again like a laser reading a barcode, presumably taking in my expensive jacket, my well-groomed appearance. Comprehension dawns on his face. "You're that rich guy from the Ark she was cleaning for."

"My name's Noah King, and yes, I run the sanctuary up the hill."

We study each other for a long moment. I can see his brain working furiously, wondering what this means.

"Aren't you going to ask how she is?" I suggest.

He doesn't say anything.

"She's well," I say. "And the baby's fine too. You're having a son, by the way."

His face shows no reaction. We could have been discussing the weather.

"What's she told you?" he asks.

"Everything." I look at his stubble-coated face, his bloodshot eyes. I can't believe Abby stayed with him so long. Her loyalty both awes and frustrates me. I know Leon has contacts at the local Women's Refuge. I make a mental note to talk to him about it. It's appalling that women stay in destructive relationships because they feel they have no way out. Men like me and Hal and Leon and Albie have to start doing something to change that.

"She told you about the money?" he says.

I nod. In the background, I hear the front door open, and behind him, I see Leon and the others coming through the door. They pause in the doorway, listening.

Tom's eyes glitter with hope. He's only concerned about the money. The thought gives me a bitter taste in my mouth.

"She's a good girl," he says. "I knew she'd help me out."

Hal and Leon exchange a glance. I glare at Tom. "She didn't ask me for the money, if that's what you're thinking."

His smile fades. "You're not giving me the money?" Panic fills his eyes. "But you don't understand, these guys, they're real mean, they break legs and stuff. I've got to pay them, or I'm done for."

I try to summon pity for him. He hasn't had the opportunities I have, the money, the loving family. Who's to say what position any of us here would be in if we didn't have the love and support and financial backing that we've had?

"I'll give you the money," I say, ignoring Hal and Leon's startled looks. I reach into my jacket pocket and pull out an envelope. "There are six thousand dollars in here. Five to pay off your debt. And enough to pay the rent for a few weeks. That's it, Tom. There's no more. If you gamble this, there'll be nobody to stand between you and those guys who break your legs."

His eyes gleam with greed. "Yeah, okay."

"And Abby's not coming back," I tell him.

He shrugs, then gives a disgusting smirk. "What did she have to do to get you to fork out that amount? I hope she was good."

"Here we go again," Albie says, and Leon says, "Shit," and strides forward, but he's too late. I'm over the sofa and on top of Tom before any of them can stop me.

I give him a sound right hook, putting all my anger and resentment behind the punch, and feeling nothing but pleasure as my fist connects with his chin. He flails his arms and one hand connects with my cheekbone, but I don't care. I punch him again, and again, until his nose crunches and blood sprays over his clothes.

"All right." Leon slides an arm beneath my elbow and lifts me up. I shake him off, wanting to mash Tom's face beneath my fist, but Hal puts a hand on my chest, moving me back, looking into my eyes.

"He's down," he says. "You got him, Noah."

I take a deep, shaky breath, then push past him, looking at the man on the floor. "Get up," I snap.

"You broke my dose!" Tom holds his hands over it. Blood trickles through his fingers.

Zach and Albie lift him up into a chair. I stand in front of him. "You're a fucking idiot," I yell at him. "Do you understand that you've lost her? She's stood by you all these years, and you've treated her like dirt, you piece of shit."

His shoulders slump. "I know." He closes his eyes. "I know."

"She's pregnant with your child, and you haven't supported her financially, physically, or emotionally. You're a sorry excuse for a man, and you make me ashamed of my sex."

Zach hands him a roll of kitchen towel. Tom takes off a couple of pieces and presses them to his nose.

"I can't help it," he whispers. "It's the gambling... I can't stop." He squeezes his eyes shut. Tears gleam on his lashes.

I look up at Leon, who rolls his eyes, and Hal, who looks pained. I reach into my jacket again and take out a card.

"This has the number of a doctor," I tell him, putting the card on the coffee table. The card bears Brock's name. I rang him this morning and discussed Tom, and he's promised to help, if Tom will accept it. "He's a good guy," I tell him, "and he has contacts with the Gambling Association, and other doctors who specialize in addiction. He'll be able to help you deal with this sickness you have. But the ball is in your court. You're what, thirty? Thirty-one?"

"Thirty-two." He coughs.

"Thirty-two—you're still a young man. You could meet someone else, have kids, have a happy life. Do you really want to spend the next thirty years like this? Drunk, penniless, and stinking like a fucking shit heap?"

He dabs at his nose. He looks a broken man, and suddenly I feel guilty for hitting him. People with addictions can't help themselves. But does that excuse the appalling way he's treated Abby?

"She's really not coming back?" he asks, his voice a whisper.

"Women are a gift, Tom," I tell him. "You should have treated her like a princess. Asked her to marry you. Worked hard to make a home for her. Given her everything she wanted. You didn't, and you've lost her. Only you can decide if you're going to make this a changing point in your life. If it's going to make you or break you."

Tears run down his face. I can't look at him anymore. I turn away. "I'm going to get her clothes. Guys, anything you see that might be hers, bag it up. Hal, keep an eye on him."

"Will do."

I pick up a bag one of them brought in and walk through to the one bedroom. Christ, this place is tiny. I open the wardrobe doors. There are surprisingly few clothes in there, and maybe four pairs of shoes. I think of the numerous racks of shoes Lisa had, and my heart twists for Abby.

I take everything out and put it into the bag as neatly as I can. Then I open the chest of drawers. Her underwear is laid out neatly, well-washed, faded, pairs of cotton panties and bras, none of the exotic items of lingerie I thought most women owned. I can't see any maternity items. I scoop it up, put it all in the bag, and go into the bathroom. The cabinet contains a makeup bag and half a dozen almost-empty bottles. I put them into a smaller bag because I don't want Tom to have them, although I'm sure she doesn't want them either.

There are no baby items around. I go back to the living room to discover that Albie has been through the kitchen and removed all her cookbooks and a few other items.

"Anyone seen the baby stuff?" I ask.

Everyone shakes their head. "I found some bottles," Zach said, "and half a dozen outfits in the corner, but that's it."

No pram or stroller? No changing mat, packs of diapers, hand-knitted blankets by family members, toys bought by colleagues and friends, beautiful onesies and funny hats, fabric books and squeaky toys?

I look at Tom, this man who took her away from her parents—which may or may not have been a blessing—away from her hometown, away from her country, to the other side of the world, who spent all her money, who made her give up her business and lost her house, who took her away from her friends, who got her pregnant, then abandoned her as if she was something he'd found on the sole of his shoe.

I want to kill him. I want to hit him until I literally pound the life out of him, and he stops breathing.

I look up and meet Leon's eyes. He looks as disgusted as I feel, but as I look at him, he gives a small shake of his head.

I turn and walk out of the door without another word.

Chapter Sixteen

Abigail

"Ooh, I've just remembered, I've got one more thing for you, hold on."

It's about an hour and a half later. We're sitting in Noah's living room, we've munched our way through the muffins, and the girls are all on their second glass of wine. I'm on lemonade, which sucks, but it's probably better I don't drink or else I'd just be bawling my eyes out constantly.

I shake my head at Summer as she gets up from the sofa and runs out to her car.

"Best to let her get on with it," Izzy says. "I've never seen her have so much fun."

I'm overwhelmed by everything the girls have brought me tonight. Summer has contacted a lot of her friends who've had babies, and she's brought everything a new mother could need, from strollers to car seats, blankets to clothing, and a diaper bag to a baby sling. I'm sensible enough to know she could easily have afforded to buy me all this new, but she was worried about offending me, and so she's passing it all off as secondhand.

Izzy bought me some beautiful white 4-ply wool because I'd mentioned to Noah that the wool I'd bought wasn't as delicate as I'd wanted. And between them, they've all chipped in and bought me a whole lot of other stuff—a breast pump, bottles, several packs of diapers, a baby monitor, and a couple of maternity outfits for me that are simply gorgeous. I changed straight into one, half-relieved and half-disappointed to take off Noah's sweater. It's a navy tunic shaped to hang over the bump, so that I look pregnant instead of just enormous. I love it. I sling Noah's sweater around my shoulders, because it comforts me, and the scent of his aftershave arises from it from time to time.

Summer comes back in, plonks herself back on the sofa, and hands me a box. "It's a night light," she says. "It throws stars on the ceiling. It's really pretty." She gives me another packet. "Not quite so exciting, but these had fallen out of one of the bags." They're breast pads. "For leakage," she says helpfully.

"They will be very useful," I advise. I've been using tissues up until now, and I know it's only going to get worse once the baby's born.

"So tell me," Nix says to Summer, her mischievous smile announcing it's going to be something saucy. "Is it true that when you orgasm, it makes you express milk?"

"Oh God, yes." Summer peels the paper off another muffin. "Zach said his calcium intake has never been so high as when I was breastfeeding." We all chortle at that. "Sometimes it squirts out," she advises. "If you try really hard, apparently you can hit the wall with it, but I never managed it."

"Jesus." Izzy rolls her eyes. "I'm not telling Hal that. He'd be determined to make it happen."

Nix snorts. "Kinky bastard."

"He's not kinky. He's enthusiastic."

"Po-tay-to, po-tah-to."

"You can talk," Remy says to Nix in her strong French accent as we all laugh. "The other day, Leon was getting grumpy because he could not find you—you had gone into town, I think. Albie told him he needed to get a pair of handcuffs and lock you to your desk. Leon said, 'Been there, done that,' and smirked."

Nix blushes beautifully as we all whoop. "Mm, well, yes, that was his birthday present."

I grin, stroking Willow's head as she comes up for a cuddle. It's been so long since I felt comfortable like this, and since I've had a proper girlie talk with women my own age. Paula is lovely, but she's quite a bit older than me, and I'd die rather than discuss sex issues with her.

"It must be really awkward having sex with a big bump," Izzy says, frowning as she tries to imagine.

"You find ways," Summer advises. "From behind is pretty cool. Bump doesn't get in the way then."

She's so frank and open. I'm a little startled by it, but it's refreshing, too. I wonder whether her illness has given her the attitude that it's pointless to be embarrassed. Why mince around delicate issues when it's so helpful to talk about things like this?

"You didn't find it put either of you off?" Nix asks. "Being pregnant, I mean?"

"Quite the opposite. Zach liked the whole womanly thing. And I found my sex drive increased, if anything. But then I don't need much encouraging when he's around." Summer chuckles and breaks off a piece of her muffin.

I laugh, feeling warm inside at being included in this group of friends, although a little envious of their relationships with their men. They all seem so happy. Will that ever happen for me? I hope so. Unbidden, I think of Noah, and the desire that sometimes appears in his eyes when he looks at me. I don't wish Peanut away, but I do wish I'd met Noah before I'd gotten pregnant. It brings such a mountain of complications, physical and emotional.

"How long have you got again?" Summer asks me.

"Eight days." I have a big gulp of lemonade. After all that waiting, suddenly it doesn't seem very long.

"If you go over, you know the best way to kick-start labor?" she winks at me.

"I thought it was having a curry," Izzy says.

"That's one way," Summer replies. "The best way is nipple stimulation, or sex. It helps to release oxytocin."

"Looks like Noah's going to be busy," Nix teases.

"Nix!" Izzy nudges her, and Remy rolls her eyes.

Nix pulls an eek face. "Oops. Sorry."

I know I must have gone scarlet because my whole face is burning. "We're not… um… an item."

"We know." Izzy glares at her friend. "And it's none of our business."

I sigh with frustration. "This is such a stupid situation."

"It's not stupid at all," Summer protests. "Noah helps people. It's what he does. He'd have helped any woman in your situation, and he'd be the perfect gentleman." She's being diplomatic, but she must read something of my feelings in my eyes, because her lips curve up. "Abby, that doesn't mean he doesn't have special feelings for you."

The other girls all laugh. "What?" I say, puzzled, as they exchange a look.

"He's head over heels," Nix says, earning herself another nudge from Izzy. "What? You told me in the car you thought the same."

"I know, but…" Izzy glares at her again and flicks her gaze at me.

Nix blows a raspberry. "I don't believe in secrets. What's the point in everyone tiptoeing around the issue? Noah's a sweetie, and there's no way he'd make a move unless he knew you were up for it, but he's gorgeous, for God's sake! And he's single, and he hasn't had sex for ten years. Jeez. The guy's going to erupt like Krakatoa when he finally gets down to it."

I cough into my lemonade, and they all burst out laughing.

"Oh my God," Izzy says, "Nix, what am I going to do with you?"

"Tell me I'm wrong," Nix demands.

Izzy purses her lips and gives me a guilty glance. "She's not. I've seen the way he looks at you. He's crazy about you. But we agreed we weren't going to discuss it because we didn't want to pile on the pressure."

I'm completely flummoxed. They all look at me and smile.

"You must have guessed," Nix says.

The feeling is mutual. Just so you know. But there's a big difference between Noah liking me, and being "head over heels." He can't be head over heels for me. Can he?

"But he'd help anyone," I protest. "Summer said that."

"Oh, Abby," Remy says. "It is not the same."

"I've known him for about twenty years," Izzy says. "I've not seen him like this with any woman since his wife died. I never thought I'd see it again."

"Do you think he just wants to recreate that part of his life?" I whisper. "Is that why he has feelings for me, just because I'm pregnant?"

"I don't believe that," Summer says. "I know he's kinda screwed up with the agoraphobia, but I don't think his grief sent him mad. He's not like that. I've known him a long time, too, and he'd be horrified to think you thought that. You make him laugh, Abby. His eyes follow you around the room. He likes you. I'm convinced of it."

I'm speechless. I stare at them, and Summer's brow creases as she glances around at her friends. "I'm so sorry," she says gently. "We really shouldn't have talked about this. I was serious when I said he's the perfect gentleman. If you're not interested him, there's no way he'd ever make a move on you, and he won't be expecting anything from you."

"It's not that," I whisper. "I do like him. Of course I do. But I'm terrified everyone will think I'm taking advantage of his kind nature. I'd hate his cousins to think I've latched onto Noah because he's rich."

"Abby, the guys are absolutely delighted," Izzy advises. "You encouraged Noah to come for a walk to the Ark. He actually drove down to the beach on his own to collect you. I don't think you truly understand what an amazing feat that was."

"And tonight," Nix continues, "he's gone out with them. He told them he'll go to the bar for a drink after they've picked up your things. Leon actually got choked up when he told me that. He worries terribly about his brother. He's thrilled that you've brought Noah alive again."

Summer reaches out and rubs my arm. "Nobody wants to say anything because you've obviously had a tough time, and you're pregnant, and we weren't sure how you felt about him. But we're all rooting for you. If the two of you got together, there'd be a parade around the Ark, I swear."

I have to swallow hard against the lump in my throat. They're giving me permission to get to know Noah? To let the relationship develop? And his cousins don't mind?

It's only now I realize how worried I am about what they think of me. I like Hal, and Albie, and Leon, and all the others at the Ark. I was hoping to get to know them all better, to have them as friends, and I was terrified they'd think I was scrounging off Noah by letting him spend his money on me.

To be frank, I'm worried I'm scrounging off him. That I've mistaken relief and gratefulness for real affection. How do you know you haven't mistaken fool's gold for real gold when you've never seen precious metal before?

But relief and gratefulness don't explain this warm feeling I have inside at the thought that he really likes me. Or the tingle I get when he looks at me with heat in his eyes.

The dogs start barking, and we look up as the door opens and the guys come in.

"Honey, he's home," Albie calls, making them all laugh and earning him a nudge in his ribs from Leon.

The girls get up, smiling as their men come forward, boisterous and argumentative as a group of teenagers. They put a few bags and boxes in the hallway, presumably containing my stuff they've managed to collect. My heart's in my mouth. Was Tom there?

"Have you been drinking?" Izzy scolds Hal as he nuzzles her neck and squeezes her butt.

"I'm driving," he reminds her. "Don't need alcohol to get me in the mood, sweetheart." He whispers something in her ear, and she gasps and smacks his arm, then laughs.

"We managed to get Noah in a bar," Albie tells us. "We had to get a couple of whiskies down him to stop him hyperventilating."

I glance across at Noah, who's giving his cousin a wry smile. I've seen men drunk enough to know Noah's far from incoherent, but his hair is ruffled and he looks… different. He turns to look at me, and it's only then I see the red mark on his cheekbone.

My eyes widen. "Oh my God. How did you get that?"

He lifts a hand to touch it gingerly and gives me a somewhat bashful look. "You should see the other guy."

Hal barks a laugh, and Leon snorts.

"Tom did that?" I'm horrified. Noah meets my eyes, then glances around the group. He doesn't want to talk about it while everyone's there.

"Come on," Summer says briskly, taking the empty wine glasses into the kitchen. "Time for everyone to go."

There's a few minutes of chaos as everyone says goodbye, kissing and giving manly bear hugs and cuddles to the dogs, and the four couples make their way to the door.

I stand in the living room, in the midst of all the bags and boxes and paraphernalia as silence descends. Noah tosses his jacket onto a chair and slides his hands into the pockets of his jeans. I stare at his bruised cheek. "What happened?"

He shrugs. "We had a difference of opinion."

"He hit you?"

"Only once."

"You hit him?"

He shrugs again. But his eyes are hard.

"What did he say?" I whisper. He shakes his head. But he doesn't have to tell me. I know what happened. Tom insulted me, probably accused me of sleeping with Noah, because he wouldn't believe a man would help me out of the goodness of his heart. And Noah decked him for it.

I look around at all the gifts I've been given by the friends of this generous man. Then I look up at him again.

I walk forward, slide my arms around his waist, and rest my cheek on his shoulder.

He takes his arms out of his pockets and puts them around me, and we stand there like that for a long, long time.

Chapter Seventeen

Noah

Over the next week, Abby and I settle into a comfortable routine.

The day after the incident with Tom, she asks if she can come on my morning walk with me. I agree, because it feels rude to say no, although part of me wonders whether I'll resent the invasion on my early morning peace. I'm surprised to find it's not a problem at all. Abby wraps up in one of my old jackets, and she doesn't chatter constantly, but seems content to enjoy the cool quietness, lost in her own thoughts.

On the third morning, I offer her a hand to help her step down onto the beach. She accepts it, and I don't know why, but I don't release it, and she doesn't take hers away, and after that we walk hand in hand every morning, as if we're the last two people alive in the world, the dogs the only witnesses to our secret, shared affection.

As we walk, I wonder—as I often have—whether Lisa is watching me. I've asked, prayed, begged, for a sign from her over the years, for her to tell me she's with me. I've never received anything. Absence of evidence isn't evidence of absence, I know that, but I'm also not convinced she's sitting on a cloud somewhere, raising an eyebrow because I'm holding hands with another woman.

And if she is watching me, I hope she understands. I miss her. I love her. I always will. But it's been ten years. I think that's enough time for any man to mourn.

In the mornings, I work in my office or occasionally have meetings, and Abby potters around the house. She still insists on cleaning, and I don't argue with her, recognizing the nesting feelings she's getting, even if she doesn't. She takes all the items Summer and the girls brought her into her room, and when I stick my head in there later, I discover she's hung the mobile above the cot, has put the nightlight on the bedside table, and has stacked all the other items neatly on a table by the window so they're at hand if she needs them.

Brock calls with the names of a couple of midwives he likes, I pass them to Abby, and she rings one and organizes for her to come to the house for a chat. After she's been, I sit Abby at the computer in the library, pull up the BabyKiwiNZ website Summer suggested, enter my credit card details, and tell Abby to order anything she needs that she doesn't have already.

She just stares at me.

"I'm serious," I tell her. "The midwife must have mentioned some things you might need."

She continues to stare at me.

I sigh. "I know it was ten years ago, but I have been there. I can vaguely remember it all. Maternity bras, breast pads, cream for cracked nipples…" I stop. She's gone completely scarlet.

"Shit," I say. "Too soon?"

We both start laughing, and she puts her hands to her face. "Oh God, Noah."

"I'm so sorry," I tell her. "I forgot we weren't married for a minute. Is this the most bizarre situation in the world or what?"

"Definitely." She shakes her head and shoots me a shy glance. "Don't take this the wrong way, but I forget how old you are sometimes."

"Oh, I am old. Positively ancient. I'll be drawing my pension soon."

She nudges me. "What I mean is, you seem like you're my age, but then I remember you're actually quite worldly wise."

"Well, sort of, for someone who doesn't go out of the house." My brow furrows. "I didn't mean to embarrass you."

"It's okay. I'm not usually easily embarrassed. It's just…" She meets my eyes, then drops her gaze again and laughs.

"What?" I say, amused.

She shakes her head and finally looks up at me again. She takes a deep breath. "It's really hard when you like a guy," she says slowly, "and you're the size of an elephant, and you feel ugly with stretch marks and leaky breasts, and you're peeing all the time and have permanent backache, and you're about to give birth to a baby who's likely to scream the place down. It doesn't exactly make you feel like a sex goddess."

It's the first time since the night I went to see Tom and she came up and put her arms around me that either of us has come close to mentioning we're attracted to one another. I've spoken to Summer privately, and she told me a little of the conversation they had—that Abby says she likes me, but she's worried everyone will think she's taking advantage of my good nature.

"She's totally fallen for you," Summer said. "But you're going to have to take it slowly, you know?"

I reach out and tuck a strand of Abby's hair behind her ear. "There's nothing ugly about pregnancy. You look amazing. Pregnancy is a beautiful thing."

Her big brown eyes stare into mine. She gives a short laugh. "Yeah, right. Because cracked nipples are soooo sexy."

"Depends on who's rubbing the cream in."

Her eyes widen. I leave it a second, then say, "Sorry, did I say that out loud?" Her lips curve up, and I laugh and get to my feet.

Summer also told me there are a few other items Abby could do with—a baby bath, wipes, a change pad or table, ointment for diaper rash, bibs, hooded towels... I wrote it all down. "You don't have to have these things," Summer advised. "But they're really helpful."

I don't just want to order them for Abby, though—I want her to have the joy of shopping for them.

"Put in an order," I tell her.

She sighs. "Noah..."

"Would it help if I showed you my bank balance?"

"That's not the point."

"I know. But it's just money. Paper and coins, sitting in a bank account. I help wounded animals, and I do my best to help wounded people, too. Please, Abby. It'll make me happy to see you getting everything you want. Do it for me."

She looks up into my eyes. "All right," she says softly.

Relieved, I leave her to it for a while. When I go back, I check the shopping cart. She's chosen twenty-nine-dollars' worth of items.

I sigh. "You're a hopeless shopper."

"I don't need anything else, Noah. I can manage."

"It's not about managing," I say, with some frustration. "Wouldn't you like to treat yourself to something pretty for the baby? Some clothes for yourself? I know Summer brought a stroller, but I'm sure you'd rather have a new one, something fancy, in bright colors?"

Abby looks up at me. Her eyes are gentle. "Noah, I honestly don't want anything else. The girls brought me lots of lovely stuff, and that was hard enough to accept. I don't feel comfortable with this. It makes me feel awkward."

That makes me sit back. I look out of the window to the Ark, although I'm not seeing the fields. I think back to when Lisa was pregnant. We were so excited, we bought everything under the sun. We spent hours in the shops, choosing strollers, cots, clothes. She loved all the little outfits and bought far too many, because they were all so beautiful.

But Abby isn't Lisa. And she's not my wife. She's not mine. Not yet, anyway. And the last thing I want to do is make her feel awkward.

I bring my gaze back to her. "I'm sorry."

"It's not that I don't appreciate everything—"

"I know." I clear my throat. "You're sure there's nothing else you absolutely need?"

"I don't think so. I got some cream for diaper rash, some wipes, and some bibs. A few other bits."

"What about for yourself?"

She hesitates. "Um, well, the only thing I saw were some nursing bras. I don't have any of those, and they do look useful."

"Sounds great. Please, add whatever you need to the cart and put the order through. Then come into the kitchen. I have a task for you."

Her lips curve up. "Thank you."

"You're welcome." I leave her to it and go back through to the living room.

Willow and Spike come up to me, and I lower myself onto the floor and give them both a bit of fuss. I feel ashamed of myself. Summer told me I need to go slow. It's only been three weeks since I first met Abby, and a huge amount has happened since then. I can't expect either of us to adjust to the situation in that short space of time.

Matt once told me, "You can't fix everyone's troubles with a wave of your wallet, Noah. All you can do is provide people with the opportunity to fix their lives themselves." They are very wise words. I gave Abby the opportunity to leave a destructive relationship, and she took it. What happens now is in her hands.

She comes out, smiling as she sees me with the dogs. "I put the order through," she says. "Thank you so much."

"You're welcome." I rise and walk through to the kitchen and beckon her to follow me.

"Noah…" She comes to stand beside me. "Did I upset you back there?"

"Of course not."

"I really didn't mean to be ungrateful."

"You weren't at all. I'm fine. More than fine. And hungry. I want you to show me how to make those apple crumble muffins that are my favorite."

She laughs. "Seriously?"

"Seriously. They're moist and crumbly, and I think you should tell someone your secret, because it would be terrible if something happened to you and the recipe was lost." I stop, realizing how that must sound, as if I'm reminding her that awful things can happen during pregnancy, and I didn't mean that at all.

But she just laughs, and nudges me with her elbow. "You must promise not to tell a soul."

"Cross my heart."

"Good. Come on, then."

We then spend a wonderful half an hour making the muffins together. Abby's happy when she's cooking, and I lean on the worktop and listen as she explains what she's doing, following her instructions when she asks me to weigh ingredients or stir the bowl.

"Peanut's so lucky," I tell her as she spoons the finished mixture into the prepared cases. "He's going to be such a fat baby with all your cooking."

She giggles. "I can think of worse things."

"Me, too." I place them in the oven for her, and she sets the timer.

"What would you like for dinner?" she asks.

I can't decide, so we peruse one of her recipe books. We both like the look of a chicken dish in a honey and mustard sauce, so we start preparing that, Abby slicing up a couple of chicken breasts, and me frying some onions and mushrooms.

"I like that you cook," she says, bringing the chicken over to the hob. "Tom never set foot in the kitchen, not unless it was to search for a packet of chips."

"I enjoy it." I take the chicken from her and add it to the pan. "Sometimes I can't be bothered, especially if I've been busy during the day, and I'll have something from the freezer, but if it's been a quiet day it's nice to spend some time on a meal."

She watches me brown the chicken, resting her hip against the worktop. "I really didn't mean to upset you."

I frown at her. "I told you, I'm not upset."

"I just want you to know… All I was saying was that I feel a bit awkward accepting money from you. You're already doing so much for me."

"It's okay."

"I don't want you to think…" She bites her lip. "That I'm not… that I don't… like you."

I look up from the pan at her. She sucks her bottom lip. It makes me want to kiss it. I want to pull her into my arms, tilt up her face, and kiss her senseless.

I don't. I do lift up the arm not holding the wooden spoon. She looks at it, her lips curve up, and she moves closer to me, sliding her arms around my waist. I place my arm around her shoulders and hug her as I stir the chicken, then kiss the top of her head.

"You make me feel better," she says, resting her cheek on my shoulder. "Just by doing this. Is that weird?"

"When you've been starved for affection, I would imagine any tender gesture is welcome," I reply.

"That's not the only reason," she whispers. "I don't want you to think that, either. I don't just like you because you're nice to me. It's much more than that."

I rest my lips on her hair. I hadn't realized until that moment how that had indeed played on my mind. Her words fill me with a rising sense of hope that it's possible there is a future for the two of us. After Peanut's born, when things return to normal.

And until then? She's close to giving birth, and I'm sure it would be weird if she wasn't somewhat scared by the prospect. If holding her like this, showing her affection, makes her feel better, well who am I to argue?

Chapter Eighteen

Abigail

The next morning, I do something I've been putting off for a while. I go into my bedroom, and I ring Tom.

Part of me doesn't want to be the one who calls. He hasn't bothered to call, text, or email since I left. But I can't escape the fact that the baby is his, and even if he's treated me badly, at the moment he has a legal right to be involved with the child.

I half hope I'll have to leave a message, but he answers, "Hello?"

"It's me," I say, heart racing. "Abby, in case you've forgotten."

He's quiet for a moment. Then he says, "I haven't forgotten."

There's a long silence. "How are you?" I ask eventually, when it appears he's not going to say anything.

"Surviving," he says. "The black eye your boyfriend gave me still fucking hurts."

Noah gave him a black eye? My lips curve up, and I have to stifle a slightly hysterical laugh.

I wait for a bit, then say, somewhat irritably, "Are you going to ask me how I am?"

"How are you, Abby?"

"I'm okay. Thanks for asking. And the baby's okay, too."

"Right."

"Do you care?"

"What do you want me to say?" he asks tiredly. "You've made your choice. I suppose we both have. You deserve better than me. I hope he gives you everything you want."

It's the first time he's ever said anything like that, and my throat tightens. "You're still the baby's father," I whisper. "I'm ringing to see whether you want to be involved."

"You mean you want money?"

I bite my lip. "Legally—and morally, most people would say—you should pay child support. But that's not what I mean. I'm talking about whether you want to be a part of his life. Do you want us to see a lawyer to discuss sharing custody?"

He's quiet for a while. I'm just about to prompt him when he says, "I'm moving back to Hamilton."

I look out of the window of the bedroom, across the fields. "When?"

"End of the week."

I'm filled with conflicting emotions. "Why?"

"Richard's offered to put me up for a while until I get back on my feet." Richard is his brother. I never liked him very much, but the two of them always got on fairly well. "I have to leave here," Tom says. "I paid the rent for two weeks, but I need to get a proper job."

"How did you pay the rent?"

"With the money he gave me."

"Who?"

"Your boyfriend," he says impatiently.

My eyebrows rise. "He gave you the money for two weeks' rent?"

"Yes, and he paid off the debt."

My jaw drops. "How much of it?"

"All of it. I assumed you knew."

"He gave you five thousand dollars?"

Tom goes quiet. Then he says, "I hate the fucking bastard with every cell in my body, but… But I'm glad you're with him. He's a decent guy, Abby. He gave me the money, and he put me in contact with a doctor who I've been talking to about the gambling."

That must be Brock. I shake my head, in shock.

"He has contacts in Hamilton," Tom says. "I'm going to join a group properly, and try to control it. I'm going to get a job. I'm not going to let it beat me. I'm… I'm sorry. For what I've done to you. You don't deserve it. You only ever gave to me, and I only ever took. I'm ashamed of that. I hope he makes you happy."

Tears fill my eyes. "Thank you."

"Once I get a job, I will send you money for the boy, I swear. And maybe sometimes you can send me a photo or something. Perhaps… in a while… I might be in a position to play a part in his life. But I can't now. I just can't. I hope you understand that."

I swallow hard, wiping my cheeks. "Yes, I understand."

"I want to be a better man, Abby."

"You will. You're a good guy at heart."

"I'm not, but I like that you think so. I hope the birth goes well. Is he going to be there?"

I can't stop the tears trickling out. "I don't know, maybe. We're not… an item. He's just looking after me."

"I'm glad. Good luck. Let me know when the baby's born."

"I will. I hope Hamilton works out."

"Me too. See you." He hangs up.

I turn onto my side on the bed. The tears continue to come, and I feel sad at the finality of the situation, but I also feel a sense of release and hope. We're done, and hopefully he'll go on to recover from his problems and be a better man.

Now, I can move on, and give all my attention, all my heart, to the baby.

When the tears stop, I go out and into Noah's office. He's on the phone, but he takes one look at my face and tells the person on the other end of the line that he'll call them back.

"What?" he asks, concerned. "Are you okay?"

"I called Tom," I say, and I tell him what Tom's said about moving away.

Noah studies my face. "Are you okay with that?"

I bite my lip. "He says you gave him the money to pay off the loan."

"Ah, yeah. I wanted to get him off your back. And although part of me wanted to kill him, I wanted to help him, too. He's sick, Abby, and he needs help." He purses his lips. "Are you angry with me?"

I swallow hard. Then I bend down and put my arms around his neck.

"Aw," he says.

I can't say anything because I'm on the verge of tears, so I just kiss his cheek.

"I know," he says, and kisses my temple. "I know."

*

Over the next week, I'm possibly the happiest I've ever been. The days are slow and gentle, and I can feel the tension of the past few months—the past few years—gradually draining away. Noah and I walk the dogs, sit and read, drink tea, make cookies and muffins together, and sometimes cook dinner together, too. Occasionally we go for a walk around the Ark, and I'm pleased to see he seems to find it easier now, and no longer has to pause on the doorstep, building up the courage. When he's working, I clean and tidy the house, play with the dogs, or sit in the library if it's raining.

Noah gives me an e-reader—he says it's an old model and he has five different ones and doesn't use this one anymore. I don't argue with him; I've wanted one for years and I'm thrilled to finally get one in my sticky paws. He leaves his account on there, complete with his credit card, and tells me to order anything I like. I don't, at first; there are more than enough free books and classics to read. But after a while, I do treat myself to a couple of books about pregnancy and birth and what to do with a newborn.

I'm so completely out of my depth. I don't have a sister or good friends who have children to talk to. I don't know what to expect, or whether the stories everyone tells you are true. All I know is that I'm coming to terms with the fact that I have a baby inside me, and it's big, and it's going to have to come out somehow. God help me.

I read the books, which give me some help, but I still have a lot of questions. I could ring the midwife, but although she was nice, it's hard sometimes to admit your ignorance to someone who's delivered a thousand babies.

I decide I'm going to be brave and I ring Summer again. She comes around after her morning's work, and we end up sitting and talking for several hours before she has to go and pick her kids up from school. She gives me lots of tips for the birth, and just makes it seem so normal, taking away some of the fear. She advises me to pack a bag now ready to go to the hospital in case baby comes early, and to make sure I know how I'm going to get there.

I haven't actually discussed this with Noah yet. I don't know if he's going to be in a position to drive me, or how he'll feel about having to spend hours there, as seems to be common. Maybe he can drop me off and then go home. Or maybe he'll order a taxi.

Later, after we've had dinner, and we're sitting together on the sofa, watching a rom-com on his big TV with a big bowl of popcorn between us, I pluck up the courage to broach the subject.

"Noah... can I talk to you about next week? About the birth?"

"Of course." His gaze is still fixed on the screen.

"I've been thinking about how to get to the hospital."

His gaze slides to me. "What do you mean?"

"Like, I was wondering whether I should get the number of a taxi firm."

He gives me a strange look. "What are you talking about? I'm taking you, obviously."

I chew my bottom lip. "What if you have a bad day?" I know some days are worse for him than others. "And labor can take hours, and I'm sure you wouldn't want to be stranded there. Maybe it would be better if I took a taxi."

He studies me with that calm consideration I'm beginning to realize means his brain is working furiously as he weighs up the pros and cons of what he's about to say. My mother used to tell me to think before I speak, but Noah is the first person I've met in real life who actually does that.

"Would you rather go in a taxi?" he asks.

I frown. "Well, no. But I'm worried about you, and—" I stop as he gives a short laugh. "What?"

"You're worried about me?" He sighs. "Honey, I'm the last thing that should be on your mind. You need to concentrate on yourself now. You need to tell me what you want, and what is best for you."

"You're never the last thing on my mind," I tell him.

His lips slowly curve up. There's a song playing in the movie, slow and romantic, and to my surprise, he gets to his feet and holds out a hand.

I raise an eyebrow. "Seriously?"

"Seriously." He flicks up the end of his fingers.

"Noah, you won't be able to get within a foot of me. And I'm clumsy, and—"

"Will you do as you're told and come here?"

I pout at him. Then I put my hand into his and let him pull me to my feet.

He turns me a little to my right so my bump is angled, slides his right arm around me, and holds my right in his left. I fit snugly under his arm, and I rest my cheek on his shoulder as we move slowly to the music.

It's been eons since I've danced with a man. Tom used to dance with me when we were younger, but it's been a long time since we've been anywhere together where music has been playing. And he would never have done this with me at home.

"I'd like to take you to the hospital," Noah murmurs. "I'd like to be there when the baby's born. Not in the room, of course, but in the hospital, so I can come and see you when it's all over."

I give a little nod. I'm not going to fight him anymore. "Okay." I can feel his jaw against my forehead, with its touch of manly stubble. He smells so nice, his lovely aftershave now mingled with the attractive scent of popcorn. I like popcorn. I like Noah. I wish it was six months later, and the baby had been born, and we were free to date like two ordinary human beings.

But we're not. I doubt there have been many more unusual situations.

"When the baby's born, I'd like to date you properly," he says, startling me. "Right now, everything's up in the air, and after what happened with Tom, I think you need time to clear your mind and decide exactly what you want. And I don't expect anything. But I would like to get to know you better."

I look up at him. "You'd take on another man's child?"

"People adopt all the time. I don't believe being a natural father automatically makes you a good father."

I remember then that he grew up with Matt King, who adopted him as his own son. Obviously, he's going to have a different view on this from a lot of other men.

It's the first time we've opened up like this, really saying what's in our hearts, and suddenly I feel it doesn't make sense to have secrets between us anymore. "Do you worry that something will happen to me like it happened to Lisa?" I ask.

"No," he says, surprising me. "I'm sensible enough to know the majority of pregnancies come to fruition without any problems. And it was a long time ago. Ten years. Christ, where has the time gone? It was another lifetime." He sighs.

"I'm sorry it happened to you," I tell him.

"Yeah. Me too. I loved Lisa. Still love her. But she's a long way back in my memory now. My feelings for her are echoes of how I felt back then, just shadows."

"So you don't think your agoraphobia is connected to your grief?"

"Not anymore. I'm sure it was. And then it sort of became its own animal. I think it was Churchill who described his depression as a black dog; well, the agoraphobia is like a snake. It coils inside me and rears up when I try to go out. It sinks its fangs into me and refuses to let go until I go back inside the house. It's insidious and cruel. But it's part of me, and I think it always will be. All I can do is try to control it as best I can. And I've been better lately. That's all down to you." He smiles.

Wow, he's so gorgeous. I love his gray hair, the creases at the corners of his eyes. And I like that he's older than me, that he's confident and self-assured. Everything about this guy makes me feel safe and cared for.

"I'm glad I could be of help," I say. His gaze slides to my mouth, and my heart misses a beat.

"Yes," I whisper. "You can kiss me." Oh God, please kiss me.

He tips his head a little to the side, his lips curving up. We're barely moving now. The music has stopped as the action continues, but I'm not aware what's on the screen. The only thing in my mind right now is the man in front of me, and the desire in his eyes.

"You're sure?" he murmurs. I nod, and so he lowers his lips to mine.

I close my eyes, giving myself over to the kiss. Mmm… I'd forgotten how wonderful it was to do this. He's so gentle, touching his lips to mine, and I sigh as he kisses across my cheekbone, over my eyebrows and eyelids, down my nose, and back to my lips. When he reaches them, he hesitates, then touches his tongue to them. I don't need asking twice. I part my lips and let him sweep his tongue into my mouth, as mine joins in the erotic dance.

He releases my hand, and I lift mine to cup his face, brushing my thumbs across his cheeks, and then slide them into his hair. Mmm… this is heavenly… His arms move around me, stroking down my back, then around the sides of my bump. It touches me, brings tears to my eyes, because it's as if he's including the baby in the kiss; he's telling me he doesn't mind that I'm pregnant. That it's not an inconvenience or something distasteful I need to get rid of before he finds me attractive. He likes me the way I am. For the first time, I glow inside at the thought of being pregnant, and see myself as beautiful.

He lifts his head and studies my face with a smile. "You're so gorgeous."

"Are you trying to make me cry?"

He chuckles. "Maybe." He looks down and strokes a hand from the top of my bump, around the side. We both laugh as Peanut kicks a foot out in response.

"He likes you as much as I do," I tell him. I feel all warm inside. He said he wants to get to know me better, that he wants to date me properly after the baby's born. It's more than I could ever have hoped for. "It's sad, isn't it," I whisper, "that we worry so much about what everyone will think of what we're doing."

"Are you worried?"

"Less than I was. The girls were nice and told me everyone's hopeful we'll get together. That your brother is pleased we're getting on so well."

His eyebrows rise. "Really?"

"Mm. That made me feel better. But we're so constrained by society, aren't we, by what we feel is right and wrong. If we went by instinct, we wouldn't have taken so long to do this, would we?"

He tucks a strand of hair behind my ear. "Maybe not. But things all happen at the time they're supposed to happen. From now on, though, I think we should forget about everyone else. I think we should do what we want, when it feels right. Does that make sense?"

I nod, wishing I could say what's in my heart—that I'd like to take him to bed, to undress him, to let him undress me, and to make love to him. I love sex, and it's been so long since it was good, and even longer since he's been with anyone. I just know he'll be great in bed, and I long to be naked with him, to have him inside me, and to give him pleasure. I haven't been with anyone except Tom since I left England with him. Don't I deserve some happiness?

But Noah's right, I suppose; it makes sense to wait until the baby's born. Peanut's muddying the waters, making me emotional, and I can see why Noah thinks it's a good idea to wait until the road ahead is clear.

He kisses me again. "For example, every time you look sad from now on, I'm going to kiss you."

I laugh, then pull the corners of my mouth down into a sad pout, and he grins and kisses me again.

"I could get used to this," I say.

"You'd better, because I'm not going anywhere." He moves back reluctantly. "Now sit down, and I'll make you a hot chocolate with whipped cream and marshmallows. How does that sound?"

"Like heaven," I say happily, taking my place back on the sofa. *I'm not going anywhere.* Those few words make me feel like a million dollars.

Chapter Nineteen

Noah

The next few days are bizarre. Abby and I are like a couple of teenagers. We're constantly kissing, and finding every excuse to bump into each other and pull the other into an embrace. She brings me a coffee in my office, leans over me to put it on the desk, and takes the opportunity to kiss my neck and then around to my mouth. I go into the kitchen when she's cooking, and while her hands are covered in flour, I slide my arms around her, stroke her bump, and tell her how beautiful she is while I nuzzle her ear.

My body feels on full alert, humming with sexual energy, which is difficult when I know there's no way I can dispose of it, save for a bit of personal DIY. But that's okay. I haven't felt like this for so long that I'm enjoying the sensation of being turned on. When you're alone for a long time, you tend to try to dampen down sexual feelings, because it's frustrating when you don't have a partner to share them with. So it feels good now to let the tiger out for a while, and watch him prowling about.

On the first day of August, it's my birthday. Abby's official due date is only two days away, so there's an air of excitement about the house. People come and go all day, bringing cards and gifts, stopping for a while to chat. The day before, Abby banished me from the kitchen, saying she wanted to prepare something for me. She brings out her present when my parents arrive late in the morning. It's a cake—the first proper birthday cake she's made since she's been here. I stare at it in delight. She's made it in the shape of an All Blacks' shirt, black with white piping, complete with the Adidas logo, the silver fern, and my name on the front with my age, forty-three, in white icing underneath. I've never seen anything like it.

"I love it," I tell her, giving her a big hug, while my parents watch and exchange glances.

They don't say anything, but later, when Abby pays one of her many visits to the bathroom, my mother says, "Things seem to be going well between you and Abby."

"Yeah," I tell them. "Very well."

Matt raises his eyebrows. "How well?"

I give him a wry look. "Dude, she's having a baby any day now."

"So? I couldn't keep my hands off your mother when she was all round and womanly."

"Matt," she scolds. "You know we're not alone in the room, right?"

I chuckle. "It's hard, but I can wait. She's had a tough time. I don't want to rush things."

To my surprise, my mother's eyes fill with tears. "I'm so happy for you," she whispers.

"Aw, Mom."

Matt pulls her to him and kisses her forehead. "It's been a long time," he says softly. "You deserve some happiness, son."

Abby comes out at that moment, and I clear my throat. "What I do deserve is a piece of cake. Although I'm reluctant to cut it because it looks so amazing." I pull out my phone and take a photo so I can show anyone who doesn't get to see it before it's devoured.

Abby grins, obviously thrilled I like it. "I'll get a knife."

We all have a piece, and everyone who visits during the day gets a slice too. Abby's thrilled to bits by everyone's compliments. It makes up a little for her persistent backache, she says.

"Not long now," Summer advises when she and Zach call in for a visit after lunch.

"I hope not," Abby grumbles. "I feel like a balloon that's been blown up too far. I swear I'm going to go pop at any moment."

"You need to try to start the labor off," Summer advises. She winks at Abby. "Remember what I said?"

Abby goes scarlet. Zach laughs, obviously in on the joke.

"We'll leave you with that thought," Summer teases, rising and coming up to give me a kiss. "Happy birthday, Noah. You know where I am if you need me."

Puzzled, I wave them goodbye at the door, then walk back to where Abby's sitting on the sofa. Her blush has died down a little, but as I approach, patches of pink appear in her cheeks again.

"All right," I say with amusement, my hands on my hips. "Out with it."

"It's just something she said that night they all came around," Abby admits. "About ways to start off labor."

"Oh?"

"Yes, um, you know, like eating spicy food and exercising…"

"And…"

She bites her lip. "I can't tell you."

I go and sit beside her, pull her into my arms, and kiss her ear. "Yes, you can."

"Oh God, Noah…" She shivers. "Summer said… um… nipple stimulation and sex encourages the release of oxytocin, and that can start contractions…" She giggles and pushes me as I start laughing. "Stop it, I'm so embarrassed."

"I'm happy to help."

"Jeez."

"Purely for scientific reasons, of course."

"Will you stop?" She gets up, somewhat awkwardly, picks up the plates, and waddles into the kitchen. "Our first sexual encounter can't be, like, a day before I give birth."

I sigh and give her a sulky look. "Why not?"

"Because! If we go to bed together—"

"When."

She gives me a wry look. "If or when we go to bed, I want to be all sultry and alluring. Not having to be lowered onto the bed with a block and tackle."

That makes me laugh. I get up and follow her into the kitchen, turn her around where she's washing the plates in the sink, and put my arms around her.

"Noah! My hands are wet."

"Don't care." I kiss her, taking my time, my lips curving up as she slides her wet hands into my hair. "You're sure I can't even interest you in an orgasm?" I murmur.

She hesitates long enough to tell me she's definitely interested, then pushes me away and carries on with doing the dishes. "Stop bothering me. I'm busy."

I laugh and leave her, but the thought plays on my mind for the rest of the day.

We have a couple of other visitors, and then it's dinner, and we decide to make an easy pasta dish together, with some homemade herb bread. We eat it out in the conservatory, talking about baby names. Abby's not made her mind up yet what she wants to call the baby, so she reads from a baby names website, getting the giggles at some of the more exotic names. "How about this—Xzayvian." She spells it out. "It sounds as if they're trying to squeeze as many consonants into the name as possible."

"It'll give him a great score at Scrabble."

She laughs. "How about Cricket?"

"As a first name?"

"Yeah."

"Well I was a pretty good fast bowler in my youth."

She's got the giggles now. "How about Burger?"

"Jesus Christ."

"Actually I prefer the name Jesus," she says, doubling over with laughter.

I chuckle and collect our plates. "Did you know that in Norway a woman was jailed for two days for naming her child Bridge?"

"Seriously?"

"Yeah. Actually she called him Gesher which means bridge in Hebrew, and Norway has strict laws regulating names. They have lists of acceptable first and last names."

"Wow. I read that a New Zealand couple called their twins Fish and Chips, but the government made them change them."

I laugh. "Those poor kids. Please tell me you're not going to call Peanut something bizarre. Like Peanut."

"I promise. I'm still thinking about it."

I roll my eyes and take the plates out to the kitchen. "Come on, let's watch a movie."

"It's your birthday," she says, following me in and taking up her usual place on the sofa. "What's your favorite movie of all time?"

"*Alien*. But I don't think that's a great one to watch when you're pregnant."

"Point taken," she agrees. "Anything else?"

"*Casablanca*."

"Aw," she says. "You're a softie at heart."

"I am. Shall we watch it?"

"Definitely."

I put the plates in the dishwasher, pick up a box of chocolates Hal and Izzy brought me around for my birthday earlier, and bring them into the living room.

I sit beside Abby, at the end of the sofa, put some pillows on my lap, and she turns and puts her legs up, leaning back so I can put my arm around her. She gives a happy sigh, and I start the movie, then offer her the box of chocolates. She chooses one and pops it in her mouth, and I have another.

The movie starts, and we settle back, enjoying the story. I feel nicely relaxed and mellow. I've had a nice day. It was good to see my folks, and everyone else who's called in today. And it's even better now, with the fire leaping, the dogs curled up at our feet, and Abby in my arms. She's wearing a pretty pale blue top and navy skirt, and her hair shines where it's spread around her shoulders. She's put on a little weight, and it suits her. She looks all glowy and feminine.

She chooses another chocolate, a Turkish delight, bites it in half, then offers me the other half. Feeling a surge of mischievousness, I hold her wrist, take the chocolate from her fingers, then suck off the small spots of chocolate that have appeared on the tip of her thumb and forefinger. I take my time, washing my tongue over her skin, and eventually her gaze rises to look at me, her lips parting and her eyelids falling to half-mast as I continue to suck.

"You're a naughty boy," she murmurs.

"Is that a complaint?"

She sucks her bottom lip. "No."

I let my lips curve up and lower them to hers.

Chapter Twenty

Abigail

We exchange a long, slow kiss, and by the time Noah raises his head, his eyes have taken on a dreamy, hazy look of desire.

"I think you should reconsider my proposal," he says.

My heartbeat immediately increases. "What do you mean?"

"I think we should try to get your oxytocin flowing."

I push him. "Stop teasing me."

He kisses my nose, then my lips again. "I'm not. The oxytocin would be a by-product. I want to give you pleasure, Abby. To make you feel good. Is that such a terrible thing?"

I stare into his beautiful violet-blue eyes. "You're serious."

"I am." He strokes my cheek, down to the hollow of my throat, and a little way down my collarbone. "You're so beautiful. You turn me on."

I don't believe him. He's just being nice. "You're pulling my leg."

Before I can stop him, he slides an arm beneath my knees and lifts me onto his lap. My jaw drops as I feel his erection beneath me. "Holy shit."

"I'll honor your wishes," he says. "I won't make love to you properly until after the baby's born. But I don't see why we can't have a little fun in the meantime." He traces a finger across my chest, just above my breasts.

God, is he serious? I want this so much. I let him kiss me, while he rests a hand on my knee, then runs it down my calf to my ankle. I sigh and lift a hand to cup his face, then slide it into his hair.

He kisses me for a long while, dipping his tongue into my mouth, until I'm breathing heavily and trembling in his arms. Then he lifts his head and kisses my nose. "Take off your bra," he says softly.

I give a short laugh, then look at his face and realize he's serious. "I'm not sure that's a good idea," I whisper. My nipples leak milk occasionally, and I can't believe any guy finds that attractive. But he nibbles my bottom lip with his teeth. My lips curve up, and then I lean forward, slide my hands behind my back, and unclip my bra. The release of the elastic is a blessed relief. "Ooh." I blow out a breath. "That's better." I extract the straps through the sleeves of my top and remove the bra without taking my top off. No way am I stripping off in front of him the first time we do anything intimate.

I drop it onto the table, then look up at him.

His erection is like an iron bar underneath me, but he ignores it and kisses me again, stroking over my shoulders, down my arms, up again, across my breastbone, between my breasts, and then he finally cups one in his hand. I inhale, and he lifts his head and watches my face as he brushes over my nipple with his thumb.

I give a helpless sigh, and he kisses me again, this time sliding his hand beneath my top. He runs his fingers across the top of my bump, then up to cup my bare breast, and his breath whispers across my lips.

"So soft…" he murmurs, taking my nipple between his thumb and forefinger and tugging it gently.

"Mmm, Noah…" I lift my arm around his neck, leaning into the kiss. As he teases my nipples, I know there's moisture forming because I can feel his fingers on the wet skin, but he doesn't stop; instead, he groans and plunges his tongue into my mouth, kissing me deeply as he brushes the moisture across my skin and continues to arouse me.

He moves from one nipple to the other, gently teasing them until my breaths come in light moans. Then he shifts his hand back to my knee and strokes up my thigh, under my skirt.

"Open your legs," he murmurs.

I part them slowly, and he continues to slide his hand up the inside of my thigh. At the top, he runs his fingers lightly over the cotton of my panties.

I sigh, so he does it again, stroking there, and I know the cotton is growing damp as my moisture soaks through it. Oh… that feels heavenly… I literally can't remember the last time someone's done this for me. He strokes me for a while, then finally lifts the elastic and slips his fingers beneath it. Gently, he parts my folds and slides two fingers down.

My head tips back and I give a long, heartfelt sigh. "Noah... Jesus. That feels... aaahhh... amazing..."

"Slowly," he scolds, giving me light strokes, teasing me, before eventually circling a finger over my clit. He's still kissing me, every now and then slipping his fingers down to tease my entrance. He doesn't penetrate me, just keeps stroking, moving from light brushes to firm strokes as my breathing turns more ragged.

"Come for me," he murmurs, lowering me back onto the pillows, and kissing down my neck to my breast. He closes his mouth over a nipple through the fabric of my top and sucks gently, stroking my clit, and I clutch my hand in his hair as my climax hits. Oh God that's fantastic, sweetly beautiful. But as amazing as the physical sensation is, I'm just as touched by the fact that he's doing this for me, that he wants to give me pleasure. My body pulses and clenches, until eventually I push his hand away.

He moves back, lifting his head to look at me.

"Oh God, oh God, oh God." I'm breathing heavily, looking up into his eyes.

He gives me a somewhat smug smile. "What?"

I shake my head, looking at him with wonder. "What do you do to me?"

He bends and kisses my lips. "It's just a taste of all the things I want to do to you once the baby's born."

I stroke his face. "Will you let me do the same for you?"

He kisses my nose. "Not tonight. It won't be long and then we'll be able to concentrate on each other. First, though, we've got to sort out little Peanut here." He strokes tenderly over my bump.

I bite my lip. "Thank you."

"For what? Making you come?"

"That as well. For making me feel beautiful."

He frowns, obviously having no idea how much that means to me. So I kiss him again. Just because.

Chapter Twenty-One

Noah

After her orgasm, Abby dozes off on my lap. I smile as I stroke her bump, feeling Peanut stir beneath my fingers. There's nothing better than giving a woman pleasure, and the wonder and delight on Abby's face at the end was a joy to behold.

Her previous relationship has obviously led her to believe she's not attractive at the moment. I hope I've been able to change her view on that a little. I sigh as I look down at the curve of her neck, the soft skin behind her ear. It would have been so easy to take her to bed, to slide into her from behind, and take my pleasure from her. Her pregnancy wouldn't have bothered me one bit. But I'm glad I waited. I don't want her to feel self-conscious or awkward when we eventually go to bed together. No matter how many times I tell her she's beautiful, Tom's treatment of her is too ingrained, and it's going to take a long time to chip away at it.

Bastard. I should have killed him when I had the chance.

She twitches and gives a little groan, presumably as she gets one of those Braxton-Hicks contractions that have been bothering her. She's had backache for a few days, and she tells me the baby has dropped, so I don't think it's going to be long.

For a brief moment, I think back to those final days with Lisa, and my heartbeat picks up. But I force the memory away. Abby will go to hospital and be in the hands of her midwife and all the trained staff. I'll pace the corridor like an old-fashioned father, waiting for news, and it'll be a straightforward birth, and everything will be fine.

I move to the edge of the sofa, gather her in my arms, and stand. She stirs and loops her arms around my neck. "Sorry, did I doze off?"

"Your snores were drowning out the TV." I kiss the top of her head.

She laughs and nuzzles my neck. "Sorry."

I take her along the corridor to her room and deposit her on her bed. "Get some rest," I instruct her. "I was thinking that tomorrow we could try filming you making muffins for the first time." We've discussed the idea of her making videos for YouTube and she's really keen on the idea.

"Okay." She smiles at me, a little shyly. "Thank you."

I lean over her and kiss her lips. "Sleep tightly, sweetheart. You know where I am if you need me."

I straighten, somewhat reluctantly. I'm tempted to suggest she shares my bed, but it's best she stays here and remains comfortable.

I go out and close the door behind me.

I stay up for a few more hours, finishing the movie and then catching up on the news, take the dogs for a short walk, then lock up the house and go to my bedroom. Spike and Willow curl up in their beds over by the window, and I get into bed.

I lie there for a while, looking out at the moon that's casting a silvery path on the Pacific. I examine my feelings to see if I feel a touch of guilt for giving Abby pleasure tonight. Part of me has always thought that if I really loved Lisa with all my heart, I'd remain a monk for the rest of my life. But I no longer think it works like that. I did love her— I still do. She'll always have a special place in my heart. But she's gone, and I'm still here. And now I have this chance to be happy again. I'd be a fool to throw that away.

I think about the moment the doctor told us the baby had died, and she was going to have to give birth to a dead baby. Even now, it makes me twist inside. She'd been too ill to hold the baby afterward. I'd cuddled my daughter for a while, tears streaming down my face, shocked at how she seemed so perfect, even though she would never draw her first breath. Giving her to the midwife to take away was possibly the hardest thing I've ever had to do in my life.

It's not going to happen this time, though. Brock's done an ultrasound, and the midwife has listened to the baby's heartbeat several times. I ask Abby every day if she's felt the baby move, and she just smiles patiently and says yes.

I'm not a curse, or a jinx. God wasn't punishing me by taking my wife and baby away. Those thoughts have been there for ten years, and I can't deny they haven't reared their ugly heads since meeting Abby.

But *que sera, sera,* and terrible things aren't going to happen just because she's with me.

I close my eyes, shutting out the moon, and refuse to open them, even though it takes me ages to get to sleep.

*

I'm awoken by Willow, whining at the door. I turn over and open my eyes, frowning as she scrapes at the frame. Lifting up, I press the button on my phone and check the time. 06:37. It's still dark, and it's unusual for the dogs to get up before I do. Willow whines again. Sighing, I blink the sleep away, swing my legs over the bed, and get up. I'm wearing my boxers, but I pull on a pair of track pants and open the door.

To my surprise, Willow doesn't turn right and head for the living room. Instead, she turns left and trots along the corridor toward Abby's room.

I follow her, puzzled. I'm halfway there when I hear Abby give a long groan.

Reaching the door, I pause a moment, then knock lightly on it. "Abby? Are you okay?"

"Noah?" She groans again. "Come in."

I open the door and go in. She's turned on the bedside light, and she's sitting back on the pillows. She rolls her eyes at me as I walk in. "Sorry. Did I wake you?"

"Willow heard you. Is everything okay?"

"I've got really bad backache. It keeps coming and going. Does that mean I'm in labor?"

My heart bangs on my ribs. I sit on the edge of the bed, trying to look calm. "Maybe. Are there any other signs?"

"No, I don't think so. It's just gotten worse and worse over the past few hours."

"Then you could well be in labor. It's probably best we take you to hospital, just in case."

She blows out a long breath, looking up at the ceiling. "Why did it have to happen at night?"

I smile. "Peanut doesn't know what time of day it is. Anyway, it's nearly morning. The sun will be up soon. Look, why don't you get dressed? I'll put the dogs out, and I'll ring the midwife and tell her."

"Okay."

"Do you need a hand?" I ask as she swings her legs over the bed.

"No, I'm okay."

"All right. I'll be back in a minute."

I go to my room, strap Spike into his chair, then take the dogs through to the conservatory. I leave the back door open for them, and give them water and a biscuit. If I end up being a while, I'll ring Leon and ask him to call in and check on them.

Moving as quickly as I can without panicking, I ring the midwife, and she says we're doing the right thing, and to meet her at the hospital. After that, I collect Abby's bag from where we keep it by the coats, add some water and a few snacks, and place it with my keys by the front door. Then I go to my bedroom to get dressed.

I'm just choosing a T-shirt when I hear her calling my name. I pull it on, run down the corridor to her room, find it empty, and realize she's in the bathroom. I open the door and my eyebrows rise as I see her sitting on the edge of the bath. Her nightie is soaked, and there's water on the floor. "My waters broke." As she speaks, she puts her hand on her bump and groans, doubling over.

"Well that answers that question," I say, pulling some towels down from the shelf. "You're definitely in labor." I lay the towels on the floor to mop up the liquid, then go into the bedroom. I open her wardrobe and rifle through the chest of drawers. "Where are your nighties?" I call out.

"I don't have any others."

I sigh and go back into the bathroom. She straightens, her wet nightdress clinging to her thighs. Her face is pale. I take out my phone, open the stopwatch, and start it going. Then I remove my clean T-shirt and pass it to her. "Take off your nightie and put this on."

She takes it without a word. I go out into the bedroom and wait for her to come out, pacing the floor. How far is it to Kawakawa? Thirty minutes or so, maybe twenty if I drive fast. It's her first child… surely she's got hours to go yet?

She comes out, wearing my T-shirt. "That's sweet of you," she says. "I'm so sorry to be so much trouble."

"Hardly. We knew this was going to happen at some point."

"Yes, but—" She stops and doubles over. "Oh God."

I help her to the bed, and then take out my phone again. It's only been three minutes since her last contraction. Holy fuck.

I sit beside her and hold her as the contraction takes her. My heart is racing. When she finally stops, I say, "Abby, they're only three minutes apart. You don't have time to go to the hospital."

She looks up at me, wide-eyed. "No, you're wrong. First babies take hours to come."

"Yes, but your waters have broken. Your contractions are three minutes apart. If we leave now, you could end up giving birth in the car."

Her bottom lip trembles. "Oh God, I'm so sorry. I didn't mean this to happen."

"It's okay."

"I can't give birth here. After everything you've been through…"

"Don't think about that."

"You don't deserve this. I shouldn't have come here…"

"Abby!" I speak firmly enough that it makes her blink. "Stop it. Babies come when they're ready, and Peanut happens to be ready now. I'm going to ring the midwife again and tell her to come here. Then we'll start getting ready, okay?"

"Okay."

I ring the midwife. I walk out as I do, trying to calm my own breathing. The last thing Abby needs is for me to panic.

"Oh dear," Claire, the midwife, says brightly. "It looks as if it's going to be a precipitate labor."

"Precipitate?"

"Fast, Noah, dear."

"But it's her first baby."

"Doesn't matter. It happens to about two in every hundred women. How has she been feeling?"

"She had backache all day yesterday, and she said it's been getting worse for a few hours."

"She's probably been in labor since yesterday, then, and just didn't realize it. It's likely to happen fast now. Typical—I'm nearly at Kawakawa. Okay, I'm turning around, but I'm going to be about twenty minutes."

"You'll be able to get here in time, won't you?"

"Hopefully. But get ready just in case. Do you have some kind of waterproof sheet for the bed?"

"Yes, I can find something."

"Hot water, lots of towels. Keep Abby moving around if she wants to. Be guided by her. Try to keep her calm."

"Who's going to keep me calm?" I try to joke, although my heart's banging like a bass drum.

"Aw," Claire says, "you're going to do just fine." We had a long chat last time she was here, and I told her about Lisa, and the strange situation with Abby. To her credit, she didn't bat an eyelid. I guess she's seen all kinds of things in her time as a midwife.

"Remember," she says, "if she feels the urge to push, she's ready to give birth. She might get a bit tearful at this point and say she needs help or that she can't do it—that just means she's in transition. Reassure her and tell her she's going to be fine. A woman's body is made for this, Noah. The baby is the right way up and everything looked fine last time I saw her. It's going to go *smooth as*. If it all happens before I get there, just do the best you can. Get her to pant to slow down the urge to push. And don't worry."

"Okay." I can hear Abby groaning again. "She's having another contraction."

"Go and get ready, then. You can ring me anytime; I'll be on speakerphone. And I'll get there as soon as I can."

"Should I ring for an ambulance?"

"I'll do that, but I'll probably get there before it. There's been a bad accident near Kaikohe, and I'm guessing the emergency services have their hands full."

"All right. Speak later." I hang up.

I stand in the corridor for a moment. I can hear Abby breathing hard as the contraction grips her. My feet are frozen to the floor.

The baby's coming. Oh Jesus. I can't do this. I think I'm the one who's in transition. How the hell can I cope with this? I can't deliver a baby. My heart is going at a million miles an hour. I feel the way I do when I'm on the doorstep, trying to take a step into the outside world. I think of Lisa, of my own baby daughter who never took a breath, and my stomach clenches in fear.

Panic overwhelms me. Holy shit. What am I going to do?

Chapter Twenty-Two

Abigail

The contraction passes, leaving in its wake a swell of panic. Oh God. I can't give birth here, on my own, in Noah's home. I can't expect him to help me. His wife died giving birth to his child. His baby died. The last thing he's going to want is to be there for me. Could I screw this up any more than I already have?

I'm sure he's trying to work out how he can extricate himself from this event without hurting my feelings. I bet he's cursing the day he invited me into his home. I should never have come here. I should have walked into the sea at Paihia and let it carry me away…

"Right." His voice makes me jump. He strides into the room with an armful of items. Glancing around, he goes over to the table by the window, plonks the items on it, and pulls it across the floor to the bed. "Time to get ready." He turns to me and puts his hands on his hips.

"I'm sorry," I whisper. "I should never have come here."

"Rubbish." He speaks gently, but he's brisk and businesslike. "It was Murphy's Law this was going to happen. I should have prepared for it. Anyway, we'll be ready when it happens. Stand up, and I'll put this waterproof sheet on the bed."

He's trying to be kind, but I know he must be hating this. I meet his eyes, and then I burst into tears.

I wait for him to exclaim impatiently, to roll his eyes, or to walk away in anger. I should have known better. He just gives a wry smile and says, "Textbook transition," and comes and sits next to me. "Hey." He takes my hand in his. "I know it's scary, but everything's going to be okay. You hear me?"

"I can't do this," I sob.

"Yes you can."

"It hurts too much. I want pain relief. I want an epidural."

He sighs. "I'm so sorry. I can't imagine the pain women go through when having a baby. I know this isn't ideal, and you must be terrified. But your body is made to get that baby out, and we're going to do it together. Do you hear me?"

I look up at him as the contraction eases. His eyes are calm.

"I don't want your first view of between my legs to have a baby's head sticking out," I wail.

That makes him laugh. "There's not much we can do about that now." He kisses my hand. "None of that matters, Abby. Nothing matters except getting Peanut in your arms, okay? This is more important than me and you. This is about a new life, about your baby boy. I've never admired anyone more than I admire you at the moment. I'm just crazy about you, and nothing is going to change that, including what happens over the next hour or so. Okay?"

His gaze is warm; I think he really means it.

Then another contraction hits me, and I double up in pain.

"Easy now," he says. "Hold my hand. We don't have any pain relief, so we're going to have to manage this with breathing techniques."

I suppose I should be annoyed with his use of 'we'—he's hardly the one trying to push a space hopper through a hole the size of a fifty-cent coin. But I like it. I don't have to go through this alone. He's going to be with me all the way, even though I have no doubt he's scared shitless. And suddenly I realize I don't care that he's going to see me at my most ungainly and awkward. It doesn't matter. I don't care what happens in the future. Right now, I need him, and he's here, at my side, holding my hand, the best friend I've ever had.

I breathe with him, exhaling with a low groan each time, which somehow seems to help. The contraction releases me, and immediately he has me on my feet so he can spread the waterproof sheet over the bed. He tosses the duvet aside, covers the waterproof sheet with a cotton sheet and then a big bath towel, and places more towels on the side. Then he comes back to me and pulls me into his arms.

"You're so brave," he says, holding me tightly. "This is going to be amazing."

"I'm scared," I tell him.

"There's no need. I'm here."

He doesn't leave my side. For the next ten minutes, as the contractions come, he holds my hand, getting me to look in his eyes as I breathe, keeping me calm. In between, I walk around the room, changing positions, trying to get comfortable, but it's impossible. The contractions are coming one after the other, one long, unbearable ache.

I sit on the edge of the bed and try to breathe through the next one, but this sensation is new and overbearing. "Noah?"

"You're doing great," he says.

"I want to push. Oh God. It can't be coming now, can it?"

"I think so. Peanut's desperate to meet you! Are you ready to see your baby, Abby?"

I lean back, trying not to panic. "I don't know what to do."

"I do," Noah says calmly. How is he so calm? "Do you want to move up onto the bed?"

"No, I want to stay here."

"All right." He gets the towels from the bed and spreads a couple on the floor. "We'll stay here." He kneels between my legs. "We need to do this as slowly as we can. I know you need to push, but keep breathing, panting if you can, to try to slow it down."

The urge to bear down is incredible, but I pant with him, feeling his hands on my tummy and legs, stroking and soothing.

"Easy now," he says. "You're doing great."

I have no idea how much time has passed… Where's the midwife and the ambulance? Outside, there's a blush of light on the horizon—dawn's coming… Ohhh… the pain is incredible… I can't believe so many women have gone through this over the last few million years…

"Keep going, sweetheart," Noah says firmly.

I breathe out, moaning softly, conscious that my body has taken over, and there's nothing I can do to stop this…

"I can see his head!" Noah's voice seems to come from far away. "He's got dark hair, Abby! He's nearly here. Keep going."

My body bears down… I'm never going to be able to do this… Oh God the pain…

And then Noah says urgently, "Stop, Abby, pant, pant," and I screw up my nose and pant… And I can feel his hands, turning the baby and guiding his shoulders out… And then all of a sudden the pain vanishes, and I collapse back onto the bed, exhausted. I've done it. The baby's out.

I lift up onto my elbows. Noah has him wrapped in a towel, and I watch, stunned, as he hooks his little finger into the baby's mouth to clear it, then rubs him with the towel… The baby coughs and takes a deep breath, and a wail fills the room…

Tears pour down Noah's face. He lifts the baby onto my chest. "You did it, Abby."

"Is he okay?"

"He's fine."

"Are you sure?"

He opens the towel to show me the baby's tiny arms and legs, the ten fingers and toes, and the bits and pieces that confirm it's a boy. "He's perfect. You've got a son, Abby. You did it!"

"We did it." I'm crying now, too. "Oh my God, he's beautiful."

"He is. He's amazing. You're amazing. I can't believe you did it."

The baby stirs in my arms, opening and closing his fingers. He has a tiny nose and a thatch of dark hair. It's my son. I have a baby boy.

I look up at Noah, who wipes a hand over his face and gives me a shaky smile. "Thank you," I whisper. "Thank you so much."

He leans forward and gives me a long, luscious kiss. "I love you," he says.

My head spins. What? He moves back and I open my mouth to reply, but at that moment he gets up as the midwife appears at the door.

"Abby!" Claire comes through, beaming with delight at the sight of the baby in my arms. "You did it!"

"I did. Look! He's so beautiful."

"He is. You clever girl." She kisses my cheek, then turns and reaches up to kiss Noah. "Well done, lad."

"*Easy as*," he says, although when he runs a hand through his hair, I can see it's shaking.

"You've done absolutely amazing," Claire tells him. "Now why don't you go and make us all a cup of tea, and I'll make sure everything's fine here."

He nods and gives me a last glance before he backs out of the door and disappears.

Claire looks at me and smiles. "Come on then, love. Let's check you out." She guides the baby's mouth to my breast, explaining that if he nurses, it'll help deliver the placenta, and cuts the cord. She checks me out and delivers the placenta, then helps me up and onto the bed so I can lean back on the pillows.

"Nice T-shirt," she says with a wink.

"It's Noah's," I say unnecessarily. "I didn't have a spare when my waters broke."

"I'm glad he was here to help you."

"He was amazing." I think of what he said just before Claire came in, after he kissed me. *I love you.* Was he just caught up in the moment? Full of emotion considering what happened to Lisa and his own baby? Or did he mean it?

There's no time to ask him. The paramedics turn up at that point, and they spend five minutes talking to Claire and making sure I'm comfortable before deciding they're not needed and heading off. Noah brings me a cup of tea and a couple of slices of toast, then starts ringing everyone, telling them the news. Later, he tells me he's also rung Tom, who was pleased it went well, and wishes me the best. I'm happy with that. Maybe in the future, he might want to play a part in Peanut's life, but for now I'm relieved he's gone.

Claire does all the regular checks on the baby, declares he's doing well, and runs me a bath. I soak for a little while, cleaning myself up, as she sits beside me, holding the baby and chatting.

"Everything all right in there?" Noah asks from outside the room. It makes me smile that he's just delivered my baby, and yet he's politely standing outside.

"Can I borrow another of your T-shirts?" I call out.

I hear him laugh. "Yeah. I'll go and get one."

I smile at Claire, who winks at me. "He's very fond of you," she comments.

I swirl the water with a hand. "I'm fond of him, too." I reach out and stroke a finger down the baby's arm. "So's Peanut."

"Are you going to christen him that?"

I laugh. "No. I'll tell you his real name in a minute."

Noah brings back a T-shirt, so I get out and pull it on, then go back into the bedroom. He's made up the bed again with lots of pillows, and the early morning sun is streaming through, lighting the room in gold. He's moved the crib beside the bed, but for now I hold the baby in my arms.

"I've decided what to call him," I tell them as I lean back against the pillows. I smile at Noah. "Ethan."

His eyebrows rise. "That's my grandfather's name."

"I know. Your mother told me. I think it's a lovely name. What do you think? Do you mind?"

He swallows hard and shakes his head, then comes to sit on the side of the bed. He looks down at the baby. "Hello, Ethan," he says softly.

Then he bends and kisses the baby's forehead. Ethan gives a tiny, beautiful sneeze, and we both laugh.

Chapter Twenty-Three

Noah

The next few days are incredibly busy. There's a non-stop flow of visitors, and everyone wants to stay and have a cuddle of the new baby. And of me, it seems. The guys are full of wonder at the fact that I delivered Ethan, and the girls keep giving me hugs and telling me how sweet I am. Which is okay. I'm not complaining.

Abby is one hundred percent focused on the baby, and that's fine too. I didn't expect anything else. I stay in the background, making cups of tea and coffee, bringing her meals, doing the laundry, and wondering how on earth *I* ended up as *her* housekeeper. It's an amusing thought, not a serious one. I'm happy to help, and it's nice to be super busy.

The baby seems healthy, and each night when Abby takes him to bed, I sit outside for a while, looking up at the stars, and trying not to be sad that my own daughter didn't make it. I knew this would be a difficult time, and that it would bring back memories, but I'm surprised at just how sad it's made me, considering how much time has passed.

Maybe it's because seeing Abby with the baby, and listening to what everyone's saying as they visit, has reinforced in my head that I'm not really a part of their lives. I've been kidding myself that I am, but the baby's not mine, and Abby's not my wife, or my girlfriend. It's true that the birth father doesn't appear interested in playing a role, but he could change his mind at any time, or she could, and ask him to take her back. I don't think that's going to happen, but you never know, and I feel that I have to prepare myself for it now the baby's born.

Summer comes to visit one afternoon, and she spends a couple of hours with Abby, going over the birth and talking babies. I leave them to it and go into my office to answer a few emails and to take a look at the report on the rebuilding of the Ark. I'll have to get down there at some point and see for myself how it's doing. I know Leon and the others are there if the builders have any questions, but I like to keep a hand on the reins myself.

"Hey, you."

I turn to see Summer in the doorway. "Hey." I get up to give her a hug. "How are you?"

"I'm good, thanks. Feeling better lately."

"Oh, I'm so glad."

"Yeah, it's good to be back on track. But enough about me. How are you?"

I raise my eyebrows. "I'm fine, why?"

"Just wondered." She gives me a mischievous smile, perching on the edge of my desk as I take my seat again. "Abby's just told me how wonderful you were on the night the baby came."

I pick up a pen and doodle on a notepad. "She's the one who did all the hard work."

"Aw, Noah, you're being modest. It must have been terrifying. Everyone talks about how labor can take days and there's Abby, ready to give birth in twenty minutes. Honestly. If I were you, I would've been running around waving my arms in the air like Kermit the frog."

That makes me laugh. "I nearly rang you," I admit. "As it happened, I don't think you'd have made it on time."

"It doesn't sound like it. Poor Abby. No wonder she's in shock."

"You think she is?"

"Oh, definitely. She's on a high at the moment with all the hormones flowing through her, but don't be surprised if she comes down to earth with a bump in a few days. She said Ethan's been good so far, but there will be days, and more likely nights, where he won't settle, and she'll need you then."

I look out of the window, filled with conflicting emotions.

"Are you okay?" she asks softly.

I nod. "It was always going to be odd. It's just stirred everything up a bit."

"That's understandable. I can see why you'd feel sad with everything you've been through. But don't let it get to you too much, Noah. Abby said she's hardly seen you since the birth—that you bring her tea and then disappear again. Have you held Ethan since he was born?"

I haven't, but I'm not going to admit that to Summer. "I've just given her a bit of space, that's all. I don't want to be hanging around her as if I'm the father."

"Maybe she wants you to hang around."

I give her a wry look. "Stop meddling."

"I like meddling. You two are made for each other, and you're going to get together—it's obvious. But I think you need a little help."

"We really don't. If it's meant to happen, it will, in time. She's got enough on her plate at the moment, Summer, looking after a newborn, without having to think about romance and pleasing me."

She purses her lips, and I wait for her to argue with me, but she just says, "All right, that's fair enough. As long as you know I'm not giving up."

"I'd never think that."

She sticks her tongue out at me. "All right, I'm off to the Ark. I'm going to do a few hours' work this afternoon."

"Don't overdo it."

"Yes, Dad."

I roll my eyes and watch her go to the door. She pauses there and turns to face me. "Ethan, eh?"

I smile.

"And you think she's not interested in you," she murmurs.

"Get lost," I scold her. "I'm busy."

She grins and disappears around the corner.

I turn back to my work, putting everything else to the back of my mind. There's no point in stewing on it. I'm here if Abby needs someone to help. Otherwise, I'll leave her to it. Lord knows she's having enough visitors. It's amazing how many women can spend hours passing the baby around and watching its every move.

*

Another couple of days pass. The midwife comes, Brock and Erin visit, then Charlie and Ophelia, and my parents visit, too. I can see how touched my mother is that Abby's chosen my paternal grandfather's name for the baby. She gives Abby a hug, then sits with Ethan in her arms while Abby tells the story about the birth once again while I make everyone tea. When Mom looks up at me, her eyes are glistening, and I know she's thinking of Lisa and the granddaughter she never got to hold.

When they go to leave, Dad gives me a long hug. "I'm proud of you, son," he says.

"I didn't do anything," I say, embarrassed.

He releases me and looks into my eyes. "Are you okay?"

"I'm fine. A bit tired." The dogs wake when the baby cries, and they wake me, so I'm sleeping in three-to-four-hourly batches at the moment.

Dad nods. "Well, take care of yourself, and of the two of them."

"I will." I let them out, thinking how strange the words are. I'm sure everyone thinks Abby and I are sharing a bed. But she's still in her room, and I'm in mine, lying there at night, thinking about her.

It's early evening, and when I go back into the living room, Abby's already yawning. "I'm going to give Ethan a bath, then go to bed, I think," she says, getting up, Ethan in her arms.

"All right." I sit in my armchair and pick up my iPad. "I hope you get some sleep."

"Thanks." She smiles, hesitates as if she's about to say something, then walks away.

I turn my attention to the book I'm reading, and refuse to think about anything else.

*

Late in the night, I'm woken once again by Willow whining at the door. I blink and sigh, roll over and check the time on my phone, and discover it's 02:47. It's pitch black outside, raining lightly. I lie there for a moment, listening. I can hear Ethan crying. His wails cut through the darkness, long and heartfelt. I sigh again, knowing Abby will put him to the breast, and then he'll quieten. I close my eyes and drift in that neverland between sleep and waking for a while.

But Willow continues to whine, and the baby continues to cry. After about fifteen minutes, I get up, pull on my sweatpants, and pad down to Abby's room, Willow at my side. Spike's still in bed; he'll be happy to stay there until I put him in his wheelchair.

Ethan's wails are louder now, and I can hear Abby talking to him. She's pleading with him to stop. And I think she's crying.

I hesitate, not wanting to intrude, but equally she doesn't have anyone else to help, and I know she must be exhausted. I knock softly on the door. "Abby?"

She falls quiet for a moment. I hear her sniffle and snuffle. Then she says, "Come in."

I open the door and go in. She's sitting on the side of the bed, and Ethan's in his cot, kicking his feet and waving his arms around as he cries. She's wearing the T-shirt I gave her on the day she gave birth. Her cheeks are wet, and she looks exhausted.

"I'm so sorry," she says. "Did he wake you?"

"Willow heard him." I walk into the room a few feet. "Is everything all right?"

"I'm so sorry I disturbed you…"

"Jesus, Abby, don't worry about that. Is the baby okay?"

"I can't stop him crying." She puts a hand to her mouth. "I've done everything they suggest—fed him, changed him, cuddled him, but he won't stop."

I walk to the cot and look down at Ethan. He's red-faced, and he looks thoroughly miserable. I look at Abby. She looks much the same. This is what Summer was talking about, I think. They're both exhausted, realizing this business of being born isn't so much fun once the novelty wears off.

I'm hardly the expert, but I don't have the hormones to deal with, and I'm not as tired as Abby. "All right," I tell her. "Let's go through everything again, step by step. First of all, why don't you change him again."

It's warm in the room, possibly a little too warm, so I go over to the windows, draw the curtains back, and open one of the windows a crack to let the cool night air lower the temperature. Abby takes Ethan over to the bed and changes him, then puts him back into his pale-green onesie.

"Try to feed him again," I tell her, "and I'll make you a cup of tea." I go down to the kitchen, leaving Willow watching them, make the tea, and return within a few minutes.

"He won't latch on," Abby says. "I only fed him an hour ago. I don't think he's hungry."

I place the tea and a couple of biscuits on her bedside table. "Could it be wind?"

"Maybe." She puts him upright over her shoulder and pats his back, but I can see she's too tired to stand. "God," she says, "I never realized I'd be quite so exhausted."

"Your body's been through a huge trauma. You just need some time to recover, that's all."

"There's no time to rest when he's feeding every few hours."

"I know. This is the time where your husband or partner should step in," I say before I can think better of it. "Tom should be helping you now."

Her bottom lip trembles, and more tears slide down her cheeks.

Shit. That was dumb. "I'm sorry," I tell her.

"I'm the one who should be sorry," she whispers. "I know I should never have left him."

I go cold inside. "You wish you were back with him?"

"No. No, that's not it at all. It's just that you don't deserve all this." She gestures around her, at the cot, the paraphernalia. "It's not your responsibility. I've taken over your house and destroyed your peaceful life."

"Only temporarily," I say with a smile, relieved she doesn't want to get back with Tom. "It's okay."

"It's not okay. I've been so selfish. What did I expect? That I'd leave Tom, and everything would fall into place? I'm so stupid."

"Right," I tell her firmly, "that's enough. You're exhausted and full of baby hormones, that's all. Everything's going to be fine. Ethan's picking up on your stress and he's upset that you're upset." I sigh. This was always going to happen at some point or other. "Give him to me."

She looks up at me, and she's so damn beautiful, her wet eyes huge in her pale face, even though she's so tired she looks as if she's about to fall over. "Are you sure?" she whispers.

"Of course I'm sure. I've left you to it for a while, but I think it's about time Ethan and I got acquainted, don't you?"

I lean forward and take the baby from her. "Drink your tea," I tell her, lifting him upright, so his cheek is resting onto my shoulder. "And have a biscuit. You need to keep your calorie intake up while you're breastfeeding."

She leans back against the pillows and sips her tea, her gaze on me.

I turn away and walk over to the window. Ethan is heavy in my arms, but so, so tiny. I stand just down from the window so he doesn't get cold, and rock him gently. He has the smallest nose, and his tiny hands are clenched into fists.

Softly, I sing to him, an old Simply Red song that's been going through my mind a lot lately, 'For Your Babies'. I used to sing it to Lisa, but it's not Lisa in my mind now, but Abby, and the beautiful baby in my arms.

Ethan cries for a while, but I have greater stamina than he does, and I'm in no hurry. I continue to sing, walking in front of the windows, while Willow lies down by the bed with her snout on her paws, and Abby sips her tea and crunches a biscuit, watching us. And gradually, Ethan quietens, and then he opens his eyes.

"Hey, dude," I murmur. "I'm Noah."

He looks up at me, his eyes big and dark blue. I bend my head and press my lips to his forehead. He smells of milk and baby powder. He's so soft and tiny. So defenseless. He blows a bubble, and I chuckle, turning back to Abby.

"He's beautiful," I tell her.

Her eyes are full of wonder. "I didn't know you could sing," she says sleepily, putting her mug back on the table.

"Hal would say I have a skill at sending people to sleep."

She smiles, her eyelids drooping.

"Go to sleep," I tell her. "I'll look after him for a while."

"I shouldn't," she says, but in less than a minute, she's dozed off.

"Come on," I whisper to Willow. She follows me out of the room and down the corridor to my own bedroom. Spike looks up as I go in and wags his tail. I smile and go over to the window where their beds are and lower myself onto the floor beside him. So far, I've kept the dogs out of the way, but I figure it's time for him to meet Ethan, too.

"Say hello," I tell him. "Nicely."

Spike nuzzles the baby and licks his hand, as Willow comes up and lies quietly beside us, her chin on Ethan's tummy. I lean back on the wall and let Ethan grab my finger, and sing to him, listening to the rain on the window.

Chapter Twenty-Four

Six weeks later

Abigail

"He's so gorgeous! Aren't you, you pretty boy?" Summer holds Ethan up and gives him a little jiggle, making him laugh. "Yes, you are! Yes, you are!" She cuddles him to her and gives a big sigh, dropping a kiss on the top of his head. "Oh, Abby, he smells so good. I love babies. I wish I could have had a dozen."

"Somewhere, Zach's passing out on the floor," I say wryly, and she laughs.

"Oh, he wouldn't have minded. But you have to be sensible, you know? I was hopeful my two boys would be grown up by the time the CF gets me. I didn't want to leave behind a baby."

She speaks so matter-of-factly, it makes me do a double take when I realize what she's said. I forget she has CF sometimes. Apart from her occasional cough, and the fact that she's quite small, there aren't many outward signs.

"Summer..." I say softly, and she waves a hand.

"Don't mind me, I'm feeling a bit wistful today. It's you, isn't it?" She kisses Ethan. "You little rascal. Brings back all the memories."

Summer took me out to lunch today, out for a drive to Kerikeri, a nearby bustling town. She drove us down to the inlet, where the old Stone Store stands that's the oldest stone building in New Zealand, and we're having a bite to eat at a small café by the river's edge.

We've become good friends over the past six weeks since Ethan was born. She started visiting me in her lunch breaks, ostensibly to have a cuddle with him, but before long we'd formed a solid friendship, and since then we've been out for lunch a few times.

"Six weeks," she says, echoing my thoughts. "It's gone so fast! Hang onto these times, Abby. I know it seems like hard work, but I swear you blink and they're ten years old."

"I know." I pass her a cloth to wipe Ethan's mouth where he's dribbled. "I do want to make the most of this. I don't know if I'll ever have another baby."

She bounces him on her knee, giving me a sideways glance. "I'm sure Noah would be open to the idea of having a baby…"

"Summer," I scold. "Stop interfering."

"Well someone's going to have to, or else the two of you will still be roommates in twenty years' time."

I sigh. Noah and I have settled into a comfortable routine I think we're both quite happy with. Ever since the night when he came into my room and took care of Ethan while I slept, he's been wonderful, looking after Ethan as if he is his own son. He changes him, plays with him, pushes the stroller when we go out for a walk, and rocks him in the evening sometimes, if Ethan gets a bit grouchy.

He hasn't mentioned our relationship, though, and neither have I. We had that brief, wonderful evening the night before Ethan was born, but since then Summer's right, we've been like roommates. He hugs me a lot, and sometimes kisses me, but they're kisses of affection more than passion. It's as if the two of us are on hold, and while it makes perfect sense to have done that, Summer's obviously picking up that I've got itchy feet.

"I know," I tell her. "Several times I've gone to say something to him, to start a conversation about the two of us, but he's really good at diverting. He'll change the subject, and I'm not sure if it's because he doesn't want me to bring us up. What if he's changed his mind? If he's decided he's not interested in getting to know me in that way?"

It wouldn't surprise me. A lot has happened since that night where he slid his fingers beneath my panties and gave me that wonderful orgasm. My body has changed significantly, for a start. And I can't forget he was present at the birth. I know some men get turned off by that, and I can't blame them. How on earth can he look at me now and see me as sexy?

But Summer shakes her head. "You forget, I'm able to watch him when he thinks you're not looking. His gaze follows you around the room. He wants you, Abby, I swear it. I think he's just wary of making a move too soon."

"If he waits any longer, I'll be tripping him up in the kitchen and doing him on the linoleum," I tell her.

She bursts out laughing. "I can think of worse ways to bump start your sex life." She hands Ethan out to me as he starts to grizzle.

I take him and put him to the breast, and he quiets immediately, kneading my boob with his fingers. I look down at him, pursing my lips. "It's not exactly the perfect time to start a relationship, is it?"

"You said Brock gave you the all clear."

"Yes…" I had my six-week check a couple of days ago. I've stopped bleeding, and Brock said everything was fine and I was doing really well. "But it would be different if Noah and I had already been dating before Ethan was born."

"True, but it's not as if you need to start dating," Summer says. "You've practically been dating ever since you've met him. You've gotten to know him really well. It's hardly going to be like a one-night stand."

I feel a little faint at the thought of having sex with Noah King. "Oh jeez. I can't, Summer. I haven't done anything like that in so long. I feel so… frumpy."

"Hmm." She narrows her eyes, and then she smiles. "I've got an idea."

Instantly, I feel wary. "What?"

"I'll tell you tomorrow," she says.

She refuses to say anything more, even after she drives me back to the Ark. She waves goodbye at the door, telling me she'll be back tomorrow afternoon, and to make a batch of cream cheese muffins for the occasion. I wave goodbye, used to her ways by now, and put it to the back of my mind.

As usual, Noah and I have dinner together, then I bathe Ethan and give him his nighttime feed as we watch a couple of episodes of a TV series. When we're done, and Ethan's starting to doze, I tell Noah I'm going to bed. He usually goes and does some work at this point, or watches a movie.

"Goodnight," he says, and gives me a hug. I'm holding Ethan, and Noah bends and kisses his cheek.

"Goodnight." I hesitate, thinking about what Summer and I talked about today, wishing I had the courage to say something, but Noah moves away and picks up our mugs to take them to the kitchen, and the moment passes. I walk along the corridor, disappointed with myself, and close my bedroom door quietly behind me. Damn it. Tomorrow, I tell myself, as I place Ethan in his cot. Tomorrow, I'll pluck up the courage and say something.

*

It turns out I'm not going to have much say in the matter. Late in the afternoon, after the Ark has closed, there's a commotion out the front of the house, and Noah goes to the door and stares as several cars draw up, and out get his cousins and their partners.

"Surprise!" Summer says brightly. Izzy and Nix are with her, and Remy, Jules, Poppy, and Clio exit from the other car. I've met them all a few times now, although this is the first time we've all been together.

"Hey," Noah says, amused. "What's going on?"

"We're going to have a girly party," Summer says. "And you," she prods him in the chest, "are being taken out for a manly drink."

He looks at Hal, who grins at him. Leon's there, too, with Albie, Zach, Stefan, Ryan, and Fitz. Clearly, Summer's been busy getting everyone organized.

"Come on," Leon says to Noah. "You haven't been out for a while. Come out with us." His eyes are gentle, encouraging. "Let's give the girls some space."

Noah hesitates, then gives in and rolls his eyes. "Okay." He glances at me. "You sure you don't mind me leaving you with this rabble?"

"I'm sure I'll manage," I tell him.

"Are there going to be muffins?" Hal asks, peering around us.

"We're going to talk childbirth and babies," Summer advises him. "In lots of gory detail."

"Eek. I'm off." He follows the others to the cars, to much laughter from the girls.

We go inside, and soon the guys' cars are heading off down the road. Summer waits for them to disappear, then takes out her phone and makes a call. "All clear," she says, then slides it back into her pocket.

I narrow my eyes at her. "What's going on?"

"You'll see," she says smugly. She ushers me into the living room.

Poppy, the ex-primary school teacher, has been coming over a lot to see Ethan, and I think we're going to be good friends. She's already commandeered him, and he's enjoying every second of being cooed over by all these young, beautiful women. The others fuss over the dogs as I take a seat on the sofa, hearing another car pull up.

"Have you ordered a stripper?" I ask, puzzled.

"Oh my God," Nix says. "We should totally have got a stripper."

Summer laughs. "Not quite, no." She goes over to the door and welcomes in a woman I haven't met before. She's carrying a large box, and as she comes in, several of the other girls wave to her.

"This is Rebecca," Summer says. "She's a beautician. She's here to pamper you!"

I stare at Rebecca, who chuckles and sits next to me. Nix is getting out a couple of bottles of wine, and they're all already tucking into the muffins I managed to make this afternoon.

"P-pamper me?" I stutter. "Why?"

"Because you deserve it," Summer says.

"And because we want to get you laid," Nix adds.

Everyone starts laughing at the look on my face, and I feel myself blushing furiously. "Summer," I scold her, "seriously!"

"Aw," she says, "come on. Every mom needs a little help sometimes to sex it up a bit."

"And we've got every bit of equipment we might need," Rebecca adds helpfully. "Shall we get started?"

I'm so taken aback, I can't think of an excuse to refuse, so I let Rebecca lead me off to the bathroom, where she de-fuzzes my legs and bikini area, gives me a facial, and pampers me with gorgeous body lotion. Then we return to the living room, where she does my nails while the girls all talk around me, fussing over Ethan and entertaining him.

"Thank you," I say to Summer. "You are such a sweetie."

"I just think it will be good for the two of you to spend some time alone together," she says. "You need to talk, Abby. That's all."

"Well, almost all," Nix adds.

"Nix," Remy scolds. "Leave the poor woman alone."

"I'm encouraging," Nix protests.

"Not everyone needs help with their love life," Jules tells her, opening another muffin.

"Says the woman who's been stalking Stefan for two years and getting nowhere," Nix announces tartly.

Jules chokes on her muffin, and the rest of us laugh as she has a couple of gulps of wine.

"I didn't realize you were interested in Stefan," I say, blowing on the nails on my left hand as Rebecca paints my right.

"I'm not!" Jules goes scarlet. "Maybe a little bit."

"He's gorgeous," Nix states, topping everyone's glasses up. "His grandfather was Swedish, so he's part Viking. He'll drag you off by your hair, Jules." She winks at her friend.

Jules covers her face with her hands. "Oh my God."

"He is lovely," I tell her. "I met his dad, too, a couple of weeks ago. He's part Maori, isn't he?"

"The best part," Nix says, "according to Elise." She laughs as Izzy elbows her and glares at her. "It's not a secret," she says. "Stefan told me himself."

"Told you what?" Jules asks.

Izzy tries not to laugh, and Nix grins. "When he was younger, Stefan's dad was a Casanova."

Everyone's eyes widen, and they all burst out laughing. I glance around at them. "What's a Casanova?"

"It's a male escort service in Auckland," Nix says. "Apparently they have excellent training."

"Holy shit," Jules says.

"I wonder whether he's passed any of his talents on to his son?" Clio says.

"Nix!"

"I'm just wondering."

"Is it true?" Poppy asks.

"It's how he met Elise," Nix says. "That's Stefan's mother," she explains to me. "Elise's friend organized a Casanova for her thirtieth birthday because she was like Noah—she hardly went out of the house. It turned out to be Stefan's dad. Elise liked him so much she booked him for a whole month, and they fell in love."

"Oh my God." I put my hand over my heart. "That's such a romantic story."

"Would it bother you to find out Hal had been a male escort?" Nix asks Izzy.

She thinks about it. "I suppose it would be weird. But then it wasn't as if Nikau hid it from her. She knew right at the beginning—that's how they met."

"I can't imagine sleeping with someone I've never met," Clio says. "I'd die from embarrassment."

"I dunno," Poppy says. "I think an escort would be fun."

"Poppy!" Remy says, and they all look shocked. Poppy doesn't tend to say much, so her announcement takes us all by surprise. Like her brother, Albie, and their father, Charlie, she finds communication difficult sometimes, so she tends to say nothing rather than put her foot in it.

"What?" she says, a little embarrassed. "I just mean it would be nice to have sex without having to get involved with someone."

Poppy told me her ex is another schoolteacher, but the relationship ended badly. Clearly, she's been scarred.

"I know what you mean," Remy says, "and I used to think the same, but I have to admit that now I am with Albie, I would miss the closeness and the support."

"And the regular sex," Jules says.

"True," Remy admits, making us all laugh. "The man is insatiable."

"It's a male King thing," Nix says. "Boundless sexual appetites." She winks at me. "I hope you're prepared."

I suddenly remember why Rebecca is there and feel a sweep of nerves. "Oh God, don't."

"Aw," Summer says. "Noah adores you, Abby. You're going to have a whale of a time."

"Remember," Nix teases, "aim the boobs at the ceiling."

"Oh dear God."

The girls laugh. "Can we give Ethan a bath?" Izzy asks. When I nod and smile, all the girls except Summer take him off to the bathroom, and soon lots of cooing noises and laughter fills the air.

Rebecca has finished my nails, and she applies a fast-drying topcoat and bids me blow on them while she starts taking her stuff out to her car.

"I've got a prezzie for you," Summer says. She holds out a bag. It says Four Seasons—the popular lingerie shop with branches all over New Zealand.

I smile wryly, open the bag, and pull out the item inside. It's the most beautiful nightdress I've ever seen. It's a plum color, made from satin with a stretchy lace bodice, and reaches down to my mid-thigh.

"Oh my God." My jaw drops. It must have cost her a fortune. "It's gorgeous."

"I've got a similar one," she says. "It's really flattering and clings in all the right places. You can keep it on, you know, if you feel a bit self-conscious."

Tears prick my eyes. "You are just the sweetest thing in the whole world."

"I want it to work," she says, hugging me. "You are two of my favorite people, and I know you're going to be perfect together."

"I'm crazy about him," I admit, hugging her back. "He's just the most wonderful man I've ever met."

"Aw." She kisses my cheek. "Tell him that, and everything's going to be all right."

I wipe my eyes, smiling as the others come back in with a squeaky-clean Ethan, and hand him to me for his last feed. I put him to the breast, but inside my heart is racing.

Is Noah still interested in having a relationship with me? Or has he changed his mind? I just hope he isn't upset by everyone interfering. Will the guys have told him what's going on? He's a grown man, when it comes down to it, older than all his cousins, and it must be embarrassing for him to think they're trying to maneuver him to go to bed with me. Maybe he'll resent the intrusion. Oh God, am I doing the right thing?

Chapter Twenty-Five

Noah

I sit in the Between the Sheets bar, sipping at my whisky, listening to the other guys talking about the rugby.

I like this bar. I used to come here years ago, back when Beck Sharpe still ran it. He's retired now, and spends a lot of time out on his boat, sailing around the Pacific Islands with his wife. Their son, Edward, has taken over the bar. It's a lot bigger than it used to be. Beck turned the cocktail bar into a restaurant, and Edward has enlarged it and made it a lot fancier. Now it specializes in seafood, fresh from the bay. We ordered a platter of nibbles to have with our drinks, and the guys are currently digging into crumbed prawns, mussels, and bite-size pieces of beer-battered fish.

I'm a little puzzled as to why we're here, but I presume it was Leon's doing, born out of a desire to make sure I don't regress and end up housebound again. I've been getting out a lot lately, walking with Abby and Ethan, and we call in at the Ark most days. I don't feel super comfortable here in town, but the old panic hasn't yet arisen, and I'm content sitting in the corner, the sounds of the sea in the distance, drinking a good Scotch.

"...won the last match against the Wallabies," Hal's saying. "I'll be disappointed if they lost this one."

"Yeah but the Aussies have a superb front row," Leon replies. "It'll be a great game on Saturday. Don't you think, Noah?"

I nod, conscious of the others glancing at me. Something weird is going on tonight, but I can't put my finger on it. "Should be a good match." I finish off my whisky. "Well, shall we get going?"

"I promised Nix we wouldn't be back before seven," Leon says, rising. "I'll get another round."

I frown as he walks off and glance at Hal. He meets my gaze over the top of his glass, but just smiles. I look at Albie, who drops his gaze to the platter and helps himself to a prawn. He's never been able to lie.

"What's going on, Albie?" I ask him.

He chews the prawn, raising his eyebrows. "What? Nothing. Nothing at all. Just eating prawns. Nothing to report."

Hal glances at him and rolls his eyes. Indignant, Albie says, "What?"

I look at Zach, then at the others. Zach sees something that fascinates him out of the window. Stefan, Ryan, and Fitz suddenly find their drinks incredibly interesting.

"All right," I say good-naturedly. "What's going on?"

"We're trying to encourage Stefan to ask Jules out," Albie says.

Stefan rolls his eyes. "For fuck's sake…"

I chuckle. "I didn't know you had a thing for Jules." It doesn't surprise me. She's young and gorgeous, and he's been single for a while.

"I don't," he says, swigging the last of his current beer.

"Why, what's wrong with my sister?" Hal demands, and we all chuckle. Stefan glares at him and leans back in his chair with a huff. Clearly, he's not going to admit it.

"Remy told me something about Jules," Albie admits out of the blue. "But if I tell you, you must swear not to do anything about it."

Stefan raises his eyebrows. "What?"

Albie glances at Hal, then at Leon as he comes back with a tray of drinks and puts them on the table. "You swear not to overreact?" he says.

"Overreact to what?" Leon hands out the drinks.

Albie mutters something to himself along the lines of "Shouldn't have started this," and then says more clearly, "You know Jules's ex, Connor?"

"Yeah," Hal says.

"He hit her."

We all stare at him. "What?" Stefan says carefully.

"Remy told me that Jules said Connor hit her," Albie says. "One evening when he was drunk. Smacked her across the face. She said she couldn't come to work that week because she had the flu, but actually she had a black eye."

"Jesus." Hal's eyes spark with anger. "I remember that."

Stefan stands up, chest heaving.

"Where are you going?" I ask him, purposely making my tone calm, even though I'm as angry as he is.

He sits down again. "Fucking bastard," he says, and bangs his fist on the table. There is definitely something Viking-esque about him. I wouldn't be surprised if he went around to Connor's house and gave him a blood eagle.

"Yeah," Albie says. "I had the same reaction. Remy had to lock the door and run off with the key to stop me going after him."

"Jules wouldn't want us to interfere," I tell them all. "I'm guessing she walked out on him afterward."

Albie nods. "Refused to talk to him. That's when she moved in with Clio. He bothered them for a bit, kept ringing and knocking on the door. Clio told Brock eventually, and he rang the police and got them to go around and give him a warning. I don't think she's heard anything from him since then."

"I'm going to tear off his balls and make him wear them for earrings," Stefan says.

"Yeah," Leon says, "you don't have any feelings for her at all."

Stefan scowls, and we all chuckle.

"I hate hearing things like that." Zach runs a hand through his hair. "It makes me angry when women talk about being afraid of all men, and then I hear something like this and I understand why."

We sip our drinks moodily, musing on the state of the male population.

"I've been thinking about working more with the Women's Refuge," I tell Leon. "I liked your idea of providing care for the animals of women who have to leave the family home because of abuse. And I thought maybe we could work with the Bay of Islands branch more closely."

"Definitely," Leon says. "We'll look into that."

"How's the Hands-On Unit coming along?" Ryan asks Albie.

"Good," Albie says. "I'm working with Poppy as she's obviously got close connections with the local primary schools. She's happy to organize trips for the kids, but she's not keen on visiting the schools herself."

"Because of Daniel?" I ask. I know she had a tricky breakup with her ex.

He nods. "Yeah. She doesn't say much, but I know what he said about her being an ice queen hurt her feelings."

Fitz stands up, mutters something, and strides off to the Gents'.

"What was that about?" I ask, amused.

"He likes her," Albie says.

"Has he asked her out?"

Albie tilts his hand backward and forward. "It's not clear. He keeps trying to initiate a conversation, but she just walks off in the opposite direction. I think she's afraid of getting hurt again."

I have a mouthful of whisky. The gruff Fitz hasn't dated anyone, as far as I know, for a year or so. I make a mental note to ask Abby whether the girls have mentioned him and Poppy at all.

"So," Stefan says. "How's Abby, Noah?" He winces then, and I suspect Zach has kicked him under the table.

I frown. "All right. It's obvious we're not just out tonight to have a drink. What's going on?"

"We're just making sure you're nicely relaxed," Hal says.

"But not too relaxed," Albie adds. "Obviously."

"Obviously," I say, even though it's not obvious at all. I glare at my brother. "Spit it out, man."

Leon sighs. "Summer wanted us out of the house, that's all. She's getting Abby…"

"Prepared," Hal finishes.

"Like a chicken for the oven," Albie says. "I don't want to know where they're stuffing the lemon."

I'm too confused to laugh, although the others all chortle, and Fitz grins as he rejoins us.

"Prepared?" I ask.

Zach sighs and leans forward on the table. "Summer thinks the two of you need a little helping hand."

My eyebrows rise. "With what?"

"You know." His lips curve up. My gaze slides to the others. They're all smirking.

Understanding dawns. "You're kidding me."

"I think Summer's hoping Abby will seduce you this evening," Hal says. "She's working on her womanly wiles."

The thought makes me feel a little dizzy. Over the past six weeks, Abby and I have skirted around one another like two ice skaters carrying out a routine. She's been warm and affectionate, and we've kissed and cuddled occasionally, but neither of us have taken that step to being more intimate. I haven't wanted to push things, unsure as to how she's feeling in both a physical and emotional sense.

"Is this Summer's idea, or Abby's?" I ask faintly.

"Both," Zach replies. "Summer says Abby watches you walk around the house as if you're a chocolate muffin."

"A stud muffin," Albie says.

"She wants to peel off your wrapper," Hal adds, and they all chuckle.

"Your face is a picture," Ryan tells me with a grin.

"I know it's been a while for you," Albie states, adding helpfully. "Want some tips?"

I lean forward and rest my forehead on the table, and they all start to laugh.

"I'm glad my love life is such a source of amusement for you all," I tell them as I sit back and have a large mouthful of whisky.

"Aw." Hal pats me on the back. "We're all thrilled for you, dude. Abby's wonderful. We just want to help."

"I think I can manage on my own, thanks," I say wryly. My mind is buzzing. How is Abby being 'prepared'? I feel all hot and bothered at the thought.

"You deserve to be happy." Leon smiles. "Not everyone could have done what you've done for her. Taken on another man's baby."

"Matt took me on," I state. "And Brock took on Ryan, and Charlie took on Summer. I think us Kings are the last people to worry about not being blood related to our fathers."

They all nod. "Good point," Albie says.

Leon checks his phone. "It's nearly seven. Come on. Time we got back."

We finish our drinks, wave goodbye to Ed, and head off. Hal's driving Albie and Stefan, and I get in Leon's car with Ryan and Fitz, and buckle myself in.

"You all right?" Leon asks as he pulls away.

"I'll be fine," I say, amused. "It might surprise you to know this, but I have done it before."

He gives me a wry look, and Fitz and Ryan snort in the back. "I didn't mean that. I mean more… you know… with Lisa…"

I look out of the window. "It's only over the past few months that I've realized how much time has gone by since Lisa died. I feel more wistful now than anything. Abby's very different from her. It's not like I'm trying to replace her."

"I know. I'm glad you found Abby. It's the main reason I agreed to tonight. I know this must be excruciating for you, but Summer's obviously desperate to help, and I kinda know how she feels."

"It's not excruciating," I say softly. "I'm touched you all care so much."

"Well it's the last time I'm ever going to get involved in your sex life," Leon advises, "so make the most of it."

We all laugh, and I feel a lifting of my spirits as he takes the turning for the Ark and heads up the hill.

I would have said something to Abby eventually. But maybe they're right, and we did need a little push.

She thinks of me like a chocolate muffin?

She really wants to sleep with me tonight?

He follows the drive around to the front of my house and parks. Hal pulls in beside him, and we get out and head for the door. I go in, bending to greet the dogs as they run up.

"Hey," Summer says, coming up as I straighten.

"Hello." I meet her gaze, and she gives me a mischievous smile.

"We're off," she says, beckoning to the others, who are all giggling like a crowd of sixteen-year-olds as they put on their coats, collect their purses, and greet the guys at the door. I'm aware of Abby joining us in the hallway and giving them hugs as they pass, but I don't look at her.

"I think we should carry you to the bed like a medieval king and queen," Hal says.

Izzy rolls her eyes and pulls him out of the door as the others all laugh.

"Bye, Noah," the girls say cheekily as they slip past me out of the door.

"Bye." I wait for the last of them to leave, then close the door behind them.

I stand for a moment, hands on my hips, listening to them as they get in their cars and then pull away. Then I finally look over at Abby, and we both start laughing.

"I am so sorry," she says, bending to ruffle Willow's ears. "I swear I didn't know they were going to do this."

"I feel as if I'm eighteen again," I tell her, closing the distance between us.

"I know, again, so sorry." She straightens and meets my eyes. Her cheeks have a slight flush. "They meant well. Summer just wanted to encourage us to talk. I suppose she's right, we should talk about us, I mean, it's easy to let time slip by, and to assume the other person isn't interested because of that, and sometimes you just need—"

I cup her face with my hands, and she stops speaking. Smiling, I lower my lips to hers.

Her mouth is soft, and she sighs and rests her hands on my chest, leaning into the kiss. I've spent so long keeping a tight rein on any lustful thoughts that it feels strange to give in to them for once. Desires flares inside me, and I slide my arms around her and hold her tightly, enjoying every second of touching her in such an intimate way after being friends for so long.

"Mmm," she murmurs when I eventually pull back. "You taste of whisky."

"Sorry."

"No, it's lovely." She licks her lips. "I haven't had a drink for so long."

I laugh and kiss her cheek, her nose, and back to her mouth. "You want to talk?" I ask her.

She shakes her head. "Not really."

"Good." I bend and lift her, and she squeals and wraps her legs around my waist as I carry her off to the bedroom.

Chapter Twenty-Six

Abigail

"Where's Ethan?" Noah asks as he turns in to the corridor toward the bedrooms.

I kiss him, threading my hands through his hair. "The girls bathed him and played with him and wore him out. I fed him and put him to bed. We should have a couple of hours' peace."

"I'll probably only need five minutes," he says, "but thanks for the vote of confidence."

We both laugh, and he stops outside his room, pushes me up against the wall, and kisses me back, delving his tongue into my mouth. My heart bangs against my ribs, and I give a low moan and tighten my fingers in his hair.

"Whose room?" he asks when he moves back, his voice husky.

"Yours," I whisper.

"Have you got the monitor on?" he asks. "So we can hear Ethan if he wakes?"

I look into his eyes, swallowing hard. "You know I'm crazy about you, right?"

He smiles and lowers my feet to the floor. "Go and get the receiver."

I run down to my room, check on Ethan, who's sleeping soundly, and turn on the monitor. Then I pause, looking at the bag that Summer gave me, which is on the bed. What the hell. Nothing ventured…

I strip off my top, skirt, and underwear, and pull on the new nightie. Summer was right; it's a beautiful fit, clinging tight to my full breasts and waist, flaring out over my hips. I fluff up my hair, check my reflection briefly, then pick up the receiver before running back down the corridor.

Noah's in his room, turning on the bedside lights. He turns as I come in, smiling, then stops and stares at the sight of me in the new nightie.

"Wow," he says.

I put the receiver on the chest of drawers and smooth the material of the nightie down nervously. "Do you like it?"

"It's beautiful." He comes over to me and puts his hands on my hips, admiring it. "You're beautiful." He meets my eyes again. His are full of desire, and a shiver runs right down my back. "Come and get in bed," he murmurs.

"I'm not cold," I protest, but I let him lead me to the bed. He draws back the duvet and I climb on, lying back against the pillows. My heart's racing. Am I really doing this?

He stands by the side, catches hold of a handful of his T-shirt at the back of his neck, and tugs it off, then removes his jeans and socks. Wearing just his boxers, he gets in beside me and draws the duvet over us. Then he puts his arms around me and falls back so I tumble on top of him.

I laugh and stretch out along him, glowing at the feel of being so close to him, skin on skin. He's all muscles and hardness, and he smells wonderful, of whisky and aftershave and hot male. A deep hunger flares inside me; I want to eat him up, to consume him.

He smiles and strokes his hands down my back, over the silky nightie, and down to my bottom, tightening his fingers on the muscles there. His erection presses against my mound, and I sigh.

"Ah, Abby." He kisses my neck, my face, my lips. "I want you so much."

My head spins. "Have I told you I'm crazy about you?"

He strokes up my back and brings his hands forward to cup my breasts. "Really?"

"Absolutely. Desperately. Completely."

He brushes his thumbs over my nipples, and I inhale and sigh. "Is that okay?" he asks. "Not too sensitive?"

I shake my head and lower my lips to his. "Nice," I murmur.

So he does it again, keeping his touch gentle, and my body stirs, awakening in a way it hasn't for a long time, like a flower blossoming after the winter snows.

We kiss for a long time, slowly exploring one another, and then he tips me onto my back and strokes my thighs, and up between my legs, his fingers light. For ages, he just brushes my skin, taking his time, his fingers sliding through my folds, circling over my clit, and making me ache deep inside.

At the same time, I explore his body, stroking over his back, down his tight butt, and over his thighs, to where his erection strains at the fabric of his boxers. I take him in my hand, feeling how thick and hard he is, and as I stroke him, heat rises inside me, and our kisses turn hungry, demanding.

At last, I can't bear it any longer, and I tug at the boxers, pleased when he slides them down and kicks them off. He reaches over to the bedside table and extracts a condom. I'm relieved I don't have to ask him. It's unlikely I'd get pregnant while I'm breastfeeding, but it's better to be sure, as I don't think either of us is ready for that conversation yet.

He rolls the condom on, then lies back on the pillows and pulls me on top of him again. "You do it," he says. "As slowly as you like. I don't want to hurt you."

I sit astride him and guide him beneath me until I feel the tip of his erection part my folds. Then, my eyes fixed on his, I sink down slowly.

His violet-blue eyes take on a look of helpless desire, and his lips part as he gives a long, heartfelt sigh. It's been such a long time since a woman has done this with him. I rock my hips a few times, coating him with my moisture, pleased there's no pain, just pleasure at being connected with this man in such an intimate way.

"Mmm." I lean forward and kiss him. "You feel amazing." Ooh, I can feel him all the way up. Wow, that's erotic. I push up and start moving, tipping back my head and enjoying the feel of my hair tumbling down my back. I feel sexy in the nightie, and the look in his eyes makes me feel beautiful.

"Ah, Abby." His hands rest on my hips. "Ohh… that's good."

I move slowly, luxuriously, thinking how amazing it is to be making love with him after all the time we've spent together. Leaning forward, I kiss him again, then gaze down at him, looking into his eyes as I slide him in and out of me. "You lied," I whisper, bending to nibble his ear.

He groans. "What do you mean?"

"You said you'd only need five minutes."

He chuckles and slides his hands up the nightie onto my skin. "My willpower is being severely tested, believe me." He rubs his thumbs across my ribs. "This nightie is gorgeous, but do I get to see beneath it?"

I hesitate and bite my lip. "Umm…"

"I like your breasts," he explains.

My lips curve up, and I think about what Summer told me could happen. "They seem to have a mind of their own, is the only issue."

"Abby," he scolds, "are you trying to turn me on?"

I laugh, filled with love for this man. "Okay." I pull the nightie up over my head and drop it to the floor.

He sighs and cups my breasts, which, I have to admit, are more than generous at the moment, and he brushes his tongue over the tips, making me groan. Oh… it's no good. As much as I want to, I can't make this last forever.

"I'm going to come…" I whisper.

"Not yet," he says, surprising me, and, holding me around the waist, he tips me deftly onto my back, still inside me.

*

Noah

Abby stares up at me, eyes wide in surprise, and then she laughs. "That was swish!"

"I might be old, but I still have a few tricks up my sleeve." I kiss her, letting the full force of my passion flow through me, and she moans and wraps her legs around my waist.

I start moving inside her, trying to make sure I'm gentle, but it's impossible when she's filling the air with her sexy sighs. She's so soft beneath me, her beautiful breasts moving as I thrust. I brush my thumb across her nipple, and she looks down and blows out a breath as she sees a bead of milk form there. Her eyes meet mine, a little wary. I give her a mischievous smile, lower my mouth there, and suck it off.

"Oh jeez." She clenches around me. "I should have known."

"What?"

"That you'd be kinky."

I laugh and kiss her, sweeping my tongue into her mouth. "It's not kinky," I tell her. "Sex isn't about being clean and sterile. Good sex should be hot and sweaty and messy."

"Oh, God, Noah. What are you doing to me?"

MY LONELY BILLIONAIRE

"Making love to you." I kiss her neck, her ear, her jaw. "Loving you."

Her mouth is hot and hungry, and there's a sense of urgency to our movements now. I'm worried about hurting her, but she says, "Harder, honey, you won't break me," and so I lift up onto my hands and move faster, thrusting into her, and feeling warmth building deep inside me.

Jesus, I've missed this, the beauty of sex, of sharing myself with a woman, of claiming her like this, and giving her pleasure. Abby's cries fill the room—she's not shy about keeping quiet, and oh, is that a turn on.

She shudders and then clenches around me, digging her nails into my back, and I hang on just long enough to enjoy her climax before heat rushes up through me, and I come myself. Oh fuck. My hands curl into fists as my body pulses, and Abby kisses my chest, my throat, my lips, until I finally relax and sink down on top of her.

"Oh my God," she says, panting heavily. "Oh I love sex. Oh I love you."

I laugh and nuzzle her neck. "I love you, too."

"Please tell me we can do that again."

"I might need a few minutes," I advise as I withdraw and then collapse back on the bed, "but absolutely, definitely, yes, we'll be doing that again."

She giggles and turns to face me, and I pull her close and kiss her forehead. "Mmm." I dispose of the condom and then lie there, exhausted. "I feel as if I've run a marathon."

"You've used muscles you wouldn't have used for a while," she says. "You'll ache tomorrow."

"It'll be worth it, though."

"I'm glad you think so."

I turn my head and smile at her. "Was that ever in question?"

We look into each other's eyes for a long while. I study her face, so familiar to me now, with her gorgeous brown eyes, and think how fortunate it was that Paula suggested Abby work for me, else I might never have met her. How strange these things are.

I open my mouth to say something, but at that moment the receiver crackles, and Ethan's thin wail echoes in the room.

"Wow," she says. "That was good timing."

"Bring him in here," I suggest, and she nods, rises, and runs out and down the corridor.

I roll onto my side, and within seconds she comes back in and slides into the bed, the baby in her arms. We face each other, Ethan between us, and she offers him her breast, smiling as he latches on, his eyelids immediately drooping.

We lie like that for a long time, watching him, enjoying just being together, while Ethan blows bubbles and finally we all fall asleep.

Epilogue

Abigail

Two weeks later

Summer moves from side to side, bouncing Ethan in her arms. "Doesn't she look gorgeous?" She gestures with her head toward the bride currently dancing with Noah. Izzy looks absolutely stunning in her ivory gown. The breeze has caught her headdress and is making it float around her head, but she's laughing, looking like an angel on this beautiful spring day.

It's late September, the day of Izzy and Hal's wedding, and luckily the weather has been wonderful. I'm sitting with most of the gang from the Ark, having half a celebratory glass of wine and a five-minute rest before Noah comes to whisk me away again for another dance.

It doesn't surprise me at all that Hal and Izzy decided to have their wedding at the Ark. Hal wanted a big do with his family, all the staff at the Ark, and a lot of our favorite clients, saying he wanted the whole world to watch him declare his life for his new wife. The square has been transformed by ribbons, balloons, and a band. The organizers set up a huge marquee in the field where we've just finished having an amazing dinner. Horses and sheep are looking through the fence, watching the proceedings, and quite a few dogs are running around with the children, enjoying the occasion.

The ceremony was incredibly touching, carried out beneath a white canopy with the backdrop of the Pacific Ocean behind them. Izzy cried as Hal promised to love her and cherish her until death parted them, and the rest of us girls—and I think some of the guys—had a few tears, too.

Izzy's dad died when she was young, and Noah was incredibly touched when she asked him if he'd give her away. He thinks this whole affair is amazing, and he's spent the whole day helping Stefan—Hal's best man—to make sure everything goes smoothly.

I watch Noah where he's dancing in the square in front of the band, occasionally twirling Izzy away from him before bringing her back into his arms. He's an elegant man who can dance as well as he sings, and he looks gorgeous today in a dark-gray suit that complements his silvery gray hair perfectly. He's wearing a white shirt and a light-gray waistcoat beneath the jacket. I'm going to ask him to leave the waistcoat on later. Hell, maybe leave the whole suit on. I kinda like the idea of having sex with James Bond.

Summer coos to Ethan, who swats a hand at her and bonks her on the nose. "Ouch," she says, and laughs.

"He's got quite a right hook on him," Hal declares. "He gave me a black eye last week."

"He did not," I scoff.

He smiles. "Enjoying the day?"

"It's fantastic," Summer says with a sigh. "I think you've made Izzy the happiest woman in the world, Hal. Look at her."

We all follow her gaze, and I catch my breath at Izzy's radiant smile as she laughs at something Noah's said.

"If I could make her smile like that every day, I'd be a happy man," Hal comments.

"Aw." I nudge him. "You old softie."

"He takes after his dad," Brock says, coming over. Hal grins, and the two of them exchange a bear hug.

"The two of you are going to smudge my mascara," Summer scolds, sniffing.

"Wouldn't be a wedding if everyone didn't cry," Hal says cheerfully, sitting back down. He smiles as Noah leads his wife toward him. Izzy runs up, sits on her new husband's lap, and puts her arms around him, and they exchange a long, sensual smooch.

"It's shocking, the public displays of affection that happen in the workplace," Leon states, then laughs as Nix leans toward him for a kiss.

Hal grins as Izzy lifts her head, then turns his mischievous gaze on Noah. "So… have you asked her yet?"

Noah fixes him with a steady stare. "No, Hal. I haven't gotten around to it yet."

"Asked her what?" I say.

"You idiot," Leon tells the new groom.

Hal pulls an eek face. "Oops. Sorry."

Noah sighs. "Well you all interfered with my sex life; stands to reason you were going to interfere with everything else." As they laugh, he stands and holds his hand out. "Come with me."

Frowning, I slide my hand into his and let him lead me away from the table. Summer waves Ethan's hand at us, and I smile before turning my gaze to the gorgeous view toward the Pacific, which is a bright blue today, reflecting the sky.

He leads me over to a fence overlooking the field, where two horses stand grazing contentedly. Then he turns to me and takes my hands in his.

"What do you want to ask me?" I say, puzzled. "Is it about making those dog biscuits that Izzy mentioned? Because I've had some ideas about those."

"No, Abby," he says patiently. "I don't want to ask you about dog biscuits." He glances across at the table, and I follow his gaze to see everyone trying to look as if they aren't watching us. "Seems I can't do anything in private," he mumbles, and sighs.

He slides his hand into the pocket of his trousers and extracts a velvet-covered box. As my eyes widen, he opens it to reveal a ring with an enormous diamond.

"Holy shit." I stare at it.

He lowers onto one knee. I shift my gaze to his face. His violet-blue eyes are as warm as the spring sun. "Will you marry me, Abby?"

I'm completely speechless. I didn't expect this as at all. It's only been two weeks since we first slept together. True, it's been an amazing fortnight, and the two of us have spent a good portion of it in bed whenever Ethan's had a snooze. And it's true that we've known each other for several months now. And he delivered my baby. And he's a better father than Ethan's actual father. But even so. He wants to *marry* me?

He wants to marry *me*?

He's still kneeling, his expression turning a little wry now. "Abby?"

"Is this a joke?" I say. It must be something Hal and Albie have concocted.

Noah sighs and gets up. "No, sweetheart." He slides a hand beneath my chin and lifts it to look into my eyes. "Wouldn't you like to stand in front of all our friends, like Izzy did today, and promise to be with me for the rest of our lives?"

My jaw drops, and I blink rapidly. "You really want to marry me?"

"I do. I love you, Abby." He looks at the box in his hand. "I want you to wear this ring so every man who sees you knows you're mine."

"It's a diamond."

"I can't get anything past you, can I?"

"Noah, it's huge!"

"Are we still talking about the diamond?"

I'm too shocked to laugh. "But..."

"I've had an idea," he says. "I thought we could get married at Christmas, maybe go somewhere in the snow, Europe or Canada or something. We could fly everyone over there. It'd be fun."

"Europe?" I'm stunned. "You think you could get on a plane?"

"I do. I'm doing so much better," he says, and he's right; for some reason ever since we slept together, his agoraphobia has improved a hundredfold.

"And one more thing..." he adds. "About Ethan... I'd like to adopt him. I delivered him—he's practically mine anyway." He smiles. "What do you think?"

My bottom lip trembles. Then I burst into tears.

Noah blows out a breath and pulls me into his arms. "Oh dear."

There are voices behind us, and then everyone's gathering around, clapping him on the shoulder and rubbing my back as they cheer.

"She hasn't said yes, yet," Noah points out, and I throw my arms around him and bury my face in his neck.

"Yes, yes, yes!"

"There you go," Hal says.

Summer's there, too, Ethan in her arms, and Noah takes him from her, lifting him up in the air and chuckling as Ethan beams at him.

"Oh, Abby," Summer says, seeing me crying, and she gives me a big hug.

"He asked me to marry him," I say through my tears.

She laughs. "I know. About time."

I look over her shoulder at Noah. He's smiling at his father, Matt King, who's come over to hug him, and his mother, who's also in tears. She kisses Ethan's forehead, and my throat tightens again.

I've spent so long being unhappy and lonely, and now I'm being welcomed into this wonderful family. My son is going to grow up surrounded by love. "I don't know what I've done to deserve this," I tell Summer, wiping my eyes.

"We're the lucky ones," she says, as Noah turns to us and passes Ethan to me.

"We are," he says, and he leans forward and kisses me, as the seagulls cry overhead, and Hal dances with his new wife under the hot spring sun.

Newsletter

If you'd like to be informed when my next book is available, you can sign up for my mailing list on my website, http://www.serenitywoodsromance.com

About the Author

USA Today bestselling author Serenity Woods writes sexy contemporary romances, most of which are set in the sub-tropical Northland of New Zealand, where she lives with her wonderful husband.

Website: http://www.serenitywoodsromance.com
Facebook: http://www.facebook.com/serenitywoodsromance

Printed in Great Britain
by Amazon